Presents, Poison, and Peril

Misadventure and Mystery, Volume 6

Travis Cramer and Marcelina Bratz

Published by Travis Cramer, 2024.

Presents, Poison, and Peril

MISADVENTURE AND MYSTERY, CHRISTMAS SPECIAL!

By Travis Cramer
& Marcelina Bratz

Edited by Violet Cramer

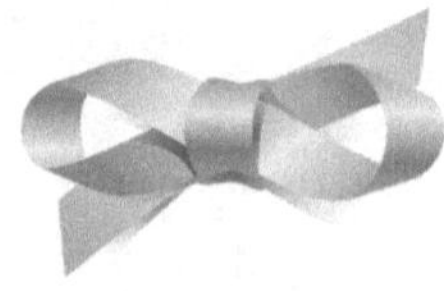

December 22nd, 3 days before Christmas

"Finally," Scott said as he shoved his last textbook into his bag, clearing out his locker. "My favorite time of the year!"

Phoebe made a face and shook her head. "I like Christmas and winter," she said. "But I don't understand why they have to close the school down. They could only close it down on Christmas Day, and it would serve the same purpose."

Scott shook his head in exasperation. "Phoebe, you are one strange bird," he said. "You may be the only person I know that doesn't enjoy school breaks."

Phoebe shrugged. "Why waste time at home when you could be learning stuff at school?"

Scott frowned. "School is a waste of time. Okay, maybe not all of it, but most of it is."

"College will eat you alive," Phoebe said dryly to Scott.

"Not necessarily," Scott disagreed. "I've been told that college isn't as rigorous as high school."

"Who told you that?" Phoebe asked. "Because you sure didn't hear it from me."

"People talk," Scott said, shrugging. Phoebe made a clucking sound with her tongue and sighed.

"Sooooo, any plans for winter break?" Scott asked Phoebe, changing the topic as the two of them began walking down the hallway.

"Family dinner," Phoebe said. "That's about it. Honestly, it's pretty much what we do every year. My parents don't switch up traditions much."

"Can't blame them, I guess. Family dinner is all we do for Thanksgiving," Scott stated.

"I can't believe everyone else ditched so early," Phoebe said, looking at the empty halls. "I think we're the last two people left in the entire school."

"Well, Remington skedaddled as soon as the bell rang," Scott said. "She was out of that class in three seconds."

"Yeah, and Adrian is on vacation," Phoebe said. "Because of course."

The Curtises went on vacation almost every holiday break. Winter break, summer break, Easter break, etc., Mr. Curtis would find every excuse to bring out the RV. Not that Adrian or Katie minded. It meant they would get an extra day off from school, since they would always leave a day before the actual break started.

"Didn't see Erica leave," Scott said. "She might still be here. Probably shooting hoops."

"Shooting hoops? It's freezing outside!" Phoebe exclaimed. "She's honestly crazy sometimes."

"Hey, she's dedicated," Scott said. "You've got to give her that. It's like you and your science projects."

"Okay, but my science projects don't involve me risking frostbite," Phoebe said sarcastically. She pushed open the large school doors and the two of them were hit with a blast of the biting winter air.

"And we get to walk home in this beautiful weather," Scott said, as the door slammed behind them. "Beautiful."

Phoebe pulled her coat closer to her chest. "I don't remember winters in North Carolina always being this brutal."

"Just wait until we get snow," Scott said. "Then it will be real fun."

"Yeah, so fun," Phoebe replied dryly. "You know, people ask me what my winter break plans are…I'm just going to sit in front of a heater and read book after book."

"Oh, and I thought you went into hibernation during winter break," Scott joked.

"Haha, hilarious," Phoebe muttered. She looked over towards the basketball court and noted two girls taking turns shooting baskets. "Who's the girl next to Erica?"

Scott turned to look where Phoebe was pointing and squinted. "I don't know," he answered. "She doesn't look familiar to me."

"Well, come on," Scott said, pulling Phoebe towards the basketball court. "Let's go introduce ourselves."

"No, come on, it's freezing," Phoebe complained. "Can't we just go home first?"

"Nope, we're going to see who she is. Come on." Scott dragged an annoyed Phoebe to the basketball court.

As they approached the court, Phoebe's annoyance grew as Scott dragged her closer to the basketball court. The cold air nipped at her skin and made her shiver.

Erica looked over her shoulder and noticed Scott and Phoebe coming toward her; she waved and waited for Scott and Phoebe to get to the court.

"Hey, Scott, hey Phoebe. This is Raven," Erica said, introducing them to the girl she was shooting hoops with.

"Hi, it's nice to meet you," Phoebe said, offering a handshake.

Raven laughed and said, "We don't shake hands in high school. Wait a few more years." She was a tall, slender girl with striking features. Her long black hair cascaded down her back, framing her darker skin with piercing, dark brown eyes. She carried herself with a quiet confidence, and her friendly smile instantly put Scott and Phoebe at ease.

"So how did you two meet?" Scott asked. Raven shared a brief story about how she had only been in town for a few days and had met Erica after school. She had shared with Erica her interest in basketball, which sparked an instant connection that led to them shooting hoops after school.

"I have to say," Phoebe said offhandedly. "You have the exact same eyes as someone else I know."

"Oh?" Raven asked. "Is that a compliment, or...?"

"Sure," Phoebe said. "I just had to mention that - sorry, it's just a habit of mine. I analyze people's faces for no reason - I guess because it helps me retain an image of them in my head."

"Cool...I guess," Raven replied, slightly confused.

Scott laughed. "Phoebe has a lot of quirks," he said. "You get used to them after knowing her for a while."

Phoebe half-scowled. "Anyway, I have to get home. I want to get started on class work, you know, for after winter break," she said.

Scott chuckled, shaking his head, "Alright, see you later." The group waved Phoebe goodbye, as she started walking home.

When she arrived home, she went inside and sat on the couch in the living room. She grabbed one of her books and was about to start reading, when she saw a small but sparkly gift under the tree.

What's this? she wondered, walking over to the tree and picking up the gift. Her parents never put gifts under the tree until Christmas Eve.

Did Remington put this here? she thought. *Or Josephine? Maybe that was why they left school so early.* The present was cleanly wrapped, with a fancy red bow tied neatly around the top, but there was no tag indicating who it was from or where it had come from.

"Should I open it?" she asked aloud to nobody in particular. She was generally against opening Christmas presents before Christmas, but her curiosity overwhelmed her, and she began to undo the ribbon on the top of the present. As she started to unwrap the ribbon slowly, she stopped for a moment.

She kept hearing a weird clicking sound, but she brushed it off as her imagination. Curiosity getting the better of her, she continued to open the gift. To her horror, the clicking sound was coming from a small bomb concealed within the wrapping. Shocked and terrified, she dropped the gift and bolted out of the living room just as the bomb exploded. Though not a large blast, it caused significant damage, leaving her disoriented and in pain. As she looked to see the damage, she felt a sharp pain in her abdomen. Phoebe realized she had been hit by shrapnel from the bomb and was bleeding profusely. Overwhelmed by the shock and the pain, she stumbled before collapsing on the floor, darkness closing in as she lost consciousness.

.. ⚜ ..

"WOW, GREAT SHOT," RAVEN said jokingly to Erica, as she chucked the ball at the net and threw it cleanly over the hoop.

Sighing, Erica retrieved the ball from the grass where she had thrown it and said, "Must be the cold."

"Sure, sure," Raven said. "Give me the ball - let me show you how to actually make a shot."

Erica laughed and tossed the ball to Raven who caught it and tossed it at the hoop, The ball banged against the blackboard and bounced back to her.

"Nice demonstration," Erica joked. Raven shook her head. "Something's up with the ball," she said, bouncing it a couple of times on the ground.

"Something's wrong with you, I think," Erica replied. "Hey, Scott, you wanna shoot a few?"

"Uh...I've never been much for basketball," Scott said. Raven tossed him the ball and Scott caught it awkwardly.

"Take a shot," Erica said to Scott. "Can't do much worse than we just did."

"I guess so," Scott said. "But if I embarrass myself, don't say I didn't warn you." Scott dribbled the ball a few times then took a shot - completely missing the basket. "Told ya so."

"No, that was...okay, yeah, no, that was terrible," Erica said, laughing. She ran over and retrieved the ball. "Wanna try again?"

"I'm good, thanks," Scott replied dryly. "We don't need to see my awful shots twice."

"Suit yourself." Erica made another throw and this time the ball bounced off the rim. "What is up with me today? I can't shoot for the life of me."

"Maybe because it's literally 30 degrees out here," Scott suggested, digging his hands into his pocket. "How long are you planning on being here, Erica?"

"I'm thinking I should leave now before I ruin any more easy shots," Erica said. "This is your ball, right Raven?" Erica tossed the ball back to Raven.

"Yeah, thanks, I'll see you around, Erica," Raven said. "And nice meeting you, Scott."

"Yeah, you too," Scott said. The two of them waved goodbye to Raven and started heading home. They walked together for a little while, until they came to the fork where their paths split.

"Alright, see ya, Erica," Scott said. Erica waved and continued down the sidewalk to her house, watching her breath cloud in the chilly winter air. She lived a few blocks away from Phoebe's house and wondered if she should stop by and say hi.

As Erica walked further down the sidewalk and closer to Phoebe's house, she was stunned to see police cars and an ambulance parked in front of it. Lights were flashing and sirens were wailing, giving her a sense of urgency and concern.

Erica ran over, and saw Officer Miles and Officer McKinley talking with Phoebe's parents. "What's going on?" Erica asked, her voice tinged with worry and confusion as she tried to make sense of what was happening. "Where's Phoebe?"

Miles looked at Phoebe's parents then back to Erica. "Phoebe's at the hospital in critical condition," she said to Erica.

Erica's heart sank at the news, her eyes widening in shock as she struggled to process the gravity of the situation. Overwhelmed with emotions, she walked away from the scene, her hands trembling as she fumbled for her phone to call Scott and deliver the devastating news. As she dialed his number, her breath hitched in her throat, each ring echoing her mounting dread of how he would react. Then the ringing stopped. Scott didn't answer.

Meanwhile, Scott was sitting in the kitchen, engrossed in a heated discussion with his parents about his low grade in algebra, completely unaware of the frantic call coming from Erica.

After Erica called Scott three more times, he finally picked up, his voice tinged with distraction as he asked what was wrong. Erica rambled off a bunch of incomprehensible words.

"Erica, slow down and say it again," he urged, his brow furrowing with concern as she breathlessly relayed the news that Phoebe was in the hospital. The words hung heavily in the air, and as the realization sank in, a wave of shock washed over him.

"I'm on my way," he replied, determination replacing confusion as he grabbed his bike and headed towards the hospital.

After he hung up, Scott hopped on his bike and pedaled furiously down the street, the cool evening air hitting his face like a wake-up call. He navigated through the familiar neighborhood, but everything felt different now—every tree and sidewalk blurred as worry clouded his mind. As he approached a busy intersection, he hesitated for a moment, glancing at the cars whizzing by, heart racing as the fear of what might be waiting for him at the hospital filled his thoughts.

Determined not to let anything slow him down, he zoomed past a red light, the adrenaline coursed through him, pushing him faster as he approached the hospital, his legs burning from the exertion but his focus unwavering.

As Erica's heart raced, she sprinted home, snatched her bike from the garage, and pedaled furiously toward the hospital, the cool wind whipping past her as she fought to keep her mind focused on Phoebe's wellbeing. As she rounded a corner, a car suddenly swerved into her lane, blaring its horn. She had to swerve sharply to avoid a collision, her pulse quickening even more from the near miss. Heart pounding, she pressed on, weaving through traffic and feeling the urgency of the moment as she finally reached the hospital's entrance.

Dismounting her bike, she hurried through the sliding doors, and burst into the waiting room. Miles and McKinley were already at the hospital, along with Phoebe's parents. "How is she?" Erica asked McKinley.

"We don't know yet," McKinley answered. "The doctors are stabilizing her now. They said that they'll let us know once she's stable."

"I don't understand - what happened?" Erica asked. "She was fine when she left the basketball court."

"A bomb," Miles responded. "At least, that's what we can assume. She was lying on the floor, bleeding, when we found her, and we found pieces of shrapnel and metal around her."

"What?" Erica asked. "A bomb? Who set it off? Why did someone want to bomb Phoebe? What kind of bomb was it?"

Before Miles could answer a single question, a nurse stepped outside and said, "Your friend is stable. We were able to remove the shrapnel from her chest - she was very lucky. Only an inch higher, and it would have gone straight into her heart."

"Where is she?" Erica asked the nurse. "Can we see her?"

"ICU, Room 145," the nurse replied. "And yes, but be warned - she's very weak. Don't stress her out."

Erica rushed down the hospital's hallway and stopped in front of Room 145. Pushing open the door, she was met with the sight of her friend lying asleep in the bed, the beeping of the monitors providing a rhythmic backdrop to the stillness, and for a moment, relief washed over her, tempered by the sight of Phoebe's pale face.

"Ugh, what happened?" Phoebe sat up feeling groggy. "Where am I?" Suddenly she heard a voice next to her, "You're awake!"

"Huh, what do you mea-?" Before she could finish her sentence, Erica bombarded her with a tight hug.

"Erica, I can't breathe," Phoebe said, trying to catch her breath.

"Oh, sorry about that," Erica said, quickly loosening her grip before pulling back to look at Phoebe. Her expression shifted from relief to concern. "But seriously, what happened? Are you okay?"

Just as Phoebe opened her mouth to respond, the door swung open and Scott rushed in, flushed and out of breath from biking to the hospital and sprinting through the corridors to find her room.

Scott hurried to Phoebe's side, concern etched across his face as he asked, "Are you okay?" Just as she was about to respond, the door swung open once more, and Phoebe's parents, Officer Miles, and Officer McKinley stepped in.

"Are you okay, Phoebe?" her mom asked, worry lacing her voice. Frustration bubbled up in Phoebe as she clenched her fists, feeling increasingly annoyed that she couldn't get a word in edgewise amid the barrage of questions and concern that surrounded her.

Feeling the weight of everyone's gaze on her, Phoebe finally snapped, "Am I going to be interrupted again, or can I actually say something?" Her voice was sharp, laced with annoyance as the frustration of being unable to express herself boiled over. "I get that you're all worried, but for once, can you just let me finish a thought without jumping in? I've been lying here, feeling completely out of it, and every time I try to explain what happened, someone else swoops in with the same question. It's like I'm not even here! I'm the one who's been through this, and I need you to listen to me for a second instead of treating me like I'm some fragile piece of glass that might shatter if you don't smother me with concern! I promise I'm okay enough to talk, but I can't do that if you keep interrupting me!"

With that, she huffed, her chest rising and falling rapidly as she looked around the room, hoping they would finally understand her need for space to process everything. She glared at the room full of concerned faces, desperate for a moment of clarity amidst the chaos.

They looked at her with shock on their faces, momentarily taken aback by the outburst. Her mother's eyes widened in surprise, while Scott's and Erica's expression shifted from concern to a mix of admiration and apprehension. Officer Miles exchanged a glance with Officer McKinley, both unsure of how to respond. The room fell silent, the tension was unbearable as Phoebe's frustration hung in the air like a thick fog. For a brief moment, the weight of her words settled in, and it became clear that beneath the worry and questions, she just wanted to be heard.

"S-sorry," Erica said quietly. "I-we didn't mean-"

Phoebe fell back into the bed, and said, "No, it's okay. It's just all very stressful. Please," Phoebe continued, taking a deep breath to steady herself, "I just need a moment to gather my thoughts before we dive into what happened."

"Take your time, Phoebe," Scott said softly, his voice filled with genuine concern as he stepped back slightly, giving her the space she needed. Phoebe closed her eyes for a moment, drawing in a deep breath as she focused on calming the whirlwind of emotions inside her, grateful for the brief silence that enveloped the room.

After another second, Phoebe opened her eyes and began, her voice shaky but determined. "I was at home, just about to start reading when I noticed a present under the tree. It was wrapped beautifully, and I got curious. I shouldn't have opened it; there was a strange clicking sound, but I thought it was just my imagination. As soon as I realized it was a bomb, I dropped it and ran, but it exploded... I didn't even see it coming." She looked around at the concerned faces. "I'm sorry for worrying everyone."

Her mother and father rushed forward, tears in their eyes. "Oh, Phoebe, I can't believe this happened to you! You're so brave for getting away."

Officer Miles nodded gravely. "You did the right thing by getting out of there. We're going to find out who did this, I promise."

Scott leaned closer; his expression serious yet supportive. "I'm just glad you're okay. We were all worried sick."

Erica added softly, "You scared us, Phoebe. Just know that we're all here for you, no matter what." Phoebe managed a small smile, feeling the warmth of their concern wash over her, grateful for their unwavering support amidst the chaos.

A nurse opened the door and said, "I hate to break this up, but visiting time is over for now."

"Of course," Scott said. "Phoebe, you should get some rest."

Phoebe smiled. "Thanks Scott - I know." She turned to the nurse and asked, "So, how long will I have to be in the hospital for?"

"We don't know for certain yet," the nurse answered. "But at least until you're mostly healed."

Phoebe nodded absentmindedly. "Yeah..." she said slowly. Erica gave Phoebe another hug - a lighter one this time - before the nurse ushered the group of people out of the hospital room and back into the waiting room.

As they settled into the waiting room, Erica glanced at Scott, her brow furrowed in concern. "Who would do something like this to Phoebe?" she asked, her voice barely above a whisper. "It doesn't make any sense. She's such a nice person; why would anyone want to hurt her?" Scott shook his head, his expression grim. "I don't know, but we need to find out. This isn't just a random attack; someone must have had a reason."

"Last time this happened, it turned out that they had gotten the wrong person," Erica replied.

"They what - oh, you mean when the Huntsmen kidnapped Josephine?" Scott asked. "And they were trying to get Remington?"

"Yeah," Erica said. "Not saying it's the case, but how do we know that Phoebe was actually the target?"

"Phoebe doesn't have any siblings," Scott replied. "Not many people you could mistake her for. And besides, they targeted Phoebe at *her* house."

"Soooo...you're saying that Phoebe has made a mortal enemy?" Erica asked. "That doesn't exactly seem like something Phoebe would do."

"Then again, she might not even know the person," Scott said.

"What?" Erica asked.

"Well, Josephine didn't know her kidnappers," Scott said.

"Yeah, but they had the wrong person," Erica said. "If we're assuming that they were targeting Phoebe on purpose, then I think it also makes sense to assume that Phoebe most likely knows of the person's existence."

"True, but we can't ignore the fact that someone went through the effort to set a trap for her," Scott replied, running a hand through his hair in frustration. "We need to figure out who had access to her house and why they would want to hurt her."

Erica rubbed her forehead. "It's winter break," she complained. "What kind of psychopath tries to kill someone during winter break - what happened to the spirit of Christmas?"

"Maybe we're looking at this the wrong way." Scott suggested.

"What do you mean?" Erica asked. "I'm pretty sure there's only one way of looking at it."

"Well, there is and there isn't," Scott said.

"Stop talking in riddles, Scott," Erica replied, annoyed. "Explain what you're saying before I lose it."

"What I'm saying is that - what if this was just a random attack?" Scott offered. "Maybe they didn't even know who they were attacking."

Erica looked at Scott as though he had just grown two heads. "That's got to be the worst suggestion ever," she said.

"Okay, well, you're welcome," Scott replied.

"No, seriously," Erica said. "Why would a person just randomly break into Phoebe's house, plant a present with a bomb in it under her tree, and then scram?"

"Look, I know it sounds far-fetched, but think about it," Scott continued, his tone more serious now. "With all the chaos in the world, it's not impossible that someone was just trying to send a message or create fear, and Phoebe happened to be in the wrong place at the wrong time."

"What's the point?" Erica asked.

"Well, no point, really," Scott shrugged, his expression troubled. "Maybe they wanted to make a statement, to show they could strike anywhere, even in a supposedly safe place like home during the holidays. It's not about Phoebe specifically; it's about creating fear in a community."

"Sounds like you're describing a serial killer," Erica said.

"No...well, actually, yes," Scott replied. "I mean, maybe not a serial killer, but..." he trailed off, unable to think of something else to say.

"They do say that serial killers like to target small towns," Erica said. "And Greensboro is pretty small."

Scott's eyes narrowed as he considered Erica's words. "What if it's someone we've already faced? Someone who has a personal vendetta against us? It's not out of the realm of possibility that this is connected to everything that happened with Josephine and those kidnappers."

"Okay, so we're hopping all over the place now," Erica said. "Is it a serial killer or is it someone we already know?"

"I don't know!" Scott said. "I'm just throwing suggestions out - I don't know what to think!"

Just then, the nurse appeared at the doorway, her expression stern. "I'm going to have to ask you all to keep your voices down or step outside," she said firmly. "Patients are resting, and we need to maintain a quiet environment. If you want to talk, be quiet."

Erica and Scott exchanged guilty glances, realizing how their escalating conversation might have disturbed the other patients.

Officer McKinley stepped forward, his tone softening as he looked at Erica and Scott "Listen, you both need to go home and get some rest. There's nothing more you can do here right now. We'll keep you updated on Phoebe's condition. You need to take care of yourselves too." Officer Miles nodded in agreement, adding, "We'll handle the investigation from here. Just stay close to your phones, alright?"

As Scott and Erica stepped outside, the cold air hit them like a wave, and they both shivered involuntarily.

"Wow, I didn't realize how late it had gotten," Scott said, glancing at his watch and frowning. "We've been in there for a while."

"Yeah, time really flew by," Erica replied, her mind still racing with thoughts of Phoebe and the chaos surrounding the situation. "I just hope she's okay. I can't believe this is happening."

The two of them walked in silence for a moment, each lost in their own worries, the tension of the day weighing heavily on them. As they turned the corner onto their street, Scott broke the silence. "Do you think we should do something? I mean, about finding out who did this?"

Erica nodded, determination flickering in her eyes. "Absolutely. We can't just sit back and let whoever did this get away with it. We need to figure out what happened, even if it means digging into stuff we might not want to."

"Right," Scott agreed, his resolve strengthening. "But first, we need to make sure we're both okay. Let's check in with our families and then regroup tomorrow."

"Deal," Erica said. "Let's meet at the library tomorrow afternoon! We can brainstorm and see if we can come up with any leads," she suggested, her voice firm with purpose.

Scott nodded, his expression serious. "Definitely. We can't just ignore this. If there's a chance that Phoebe is in danger, we need to do everything we can to help her." He paused for a moment, considering their next steps. "I'll bring my laptop so we can look up anything we can find about similar incidents or anyone who might have it out for her."

And with that, the two friends gave each other a quick hug, before heading back home to get some much-needed sleep.

December 23rd, 2 days before Christmas.

Tomorrow afternoon came quickly, and Scott and Erica arrived at the library, the air thick with anticipation and unease. They settled at a table near the back, unpacking their materials and trying to focus on the task at hand. Just as they began to sift through their notes, the door swung open, and in rushed Remington and Josephine, their faces flushed with urgency.

"Scott! Erica!" Remington called out, her voice cutting through the quiet of the library. "We need to talk!"

"What do you know?" Scott asked, standing up as they approached. The worry in his eyes mirrored that of Erica's.

What happened?" Erica pressed.

Josephine took a deep breath, her expression serious. "We heard Officer Miles speak to Officer McKinley last night. We heard everything about Phoebe... and we're really worried."

"She said it looks like someone intended to send a message," Remington explained, her voice trembling slightly. "They found traces of the bomb's components, and it was targeted."

Scott exchanged a glance with Erica, the implications weighing heavily on them. "Targeted? But why would anyone want to hurt Phoebe?"

Josephine shook her head, her eyes filled with concern. "That's what we need to figure out. Officer Miles hinted that it could be connected to something bigger. Something from the past."

"Like with Josephine's kidnapping?" Scott asked, his mind racing. "But why would they involve Phoebe?"

"We don't know," Remington admitted, frustration creeping into her voice. "But we can't just sit back and let this happen. We need to find out who is behind this and why."

Erica nodded, her resolve hardening. "We need to investigate. If Phoebe is in danger, we can't wait for the adults to figure it out."

"Exactly," Scott said. "Let's start by looking into anyone who might have a grudge against Phoebe or our families. We need to dig deeper into what Officer Miles knows."

"Do they know if the bomb was homemade?" Josephine asked.

"I don't think so," Scott said. "But if it was, that proves something. The person was skilled - they knew what they were doing."

Scott's phone began to ring and he pulled it out of his pocket. "It's Adrian," he said. "I thought he was going winter camping and wouldn't have any cell signal."

Scott stood up from the table they were sitting at and went to the room where he could answer his phone without disturbing anyone and the rest of the group followed him.

"Hey Adrian," Scott said into the phone. There was dead silence for a little bit before Adrian's voice came over the phone.

"H-hey Sco–tt." Adrian's voice was spotty and broken up. "Ju–st wan-n-nted to s-s-s-ay h-"

"Adrian, you're breaking up," Scott said.

"S-ss-orry, bad ce-" Adrian's voice cut off.

"Hello? Adrian, you there?" Scott asked. The call died and Scott shrugged. "Guess he's camping all right."

"Did any of you tell him what happened to Phoebe?" Remington asked.

"Not me," Erica said. "Didn't really think it was necessary to text him, since I figured he probably wouldn't receive the text anyway."

"Yeah, me neither," Remington added. Scott's phone began to ring again and he picked it up.

"Adrian?" he asked. "Do you have a better cell signal now?"

"I think so," Adrian replied through the phone, his voice clearer now. "Can you hear me better?"

"Yeah, much better," Scott said. "What's up?"

"Not much," Adrian replied. "There's not a lot of cell signal where I'm at - if you haven't guessed - but me and Katie climbed to the top of a hill and we got some connection from something. Only if I hold my phone in the air, though. Has anything interesting happened back at home?"

"Oh, it sure has," Remington interjected.

"Remington?" Adrian asked. "Are you guys all together?"

"Yeah, we're at the library," Josephine replied.

"So, what's going on at home?" Adrian asked.

"There was a bomb planted at Phoebe's house!" everyone said into the phone at the same time. There was silence for a while.

"What?" Adrian asked.

"There was a bomb - planted at Phoebe's house," Scott said. "She said that she found a present under her tree, and when she opened it, something inside blew up."

There was another brief moment of silence. "A bomb??" Adrian asked incredulously. "Is Phoebe alright?"

"Yes, thankfully," Remington said, leaning over Scott's shoulder and talking into his phone. "She's at the hospital - some of the bomb fragments hit her in the chest, but she's okay."

"That's good," Adrian said simply. More silence. "Sorry, that is a lot to take in while you're standing on top of a snowy mountain."

"No kidding," Erica said.

"Okay, do Miles or McKinley know who set the bomb?" Adrian asked.

"No, or at least, if they do, they haven't told us," Josephine answered.

"This is crazy news, guys, but I have to say it is literally freezing up on this mountain, and I think my parents are signaling for me and

Katie to come down," Adrian said. "But, uh, keep me updated as best as possible. I won't always be able to check my texts, but I'll respond when I can."

"Okay, see ya later," Scott said to Adrian. "Have fun on the rest of your camping trip."

"Yeah, thanks man," Adrian replied, before hanging up the phone. Scott put his phone back in his pocket and asked the rest of the group, "Okay, what are we doing here again?"

"Pooling what little information we know," Remington replied, stepping outside of the phone call room. They took a seat at the table again and Scott pulled out a notebook.

"Let's brainstorm," he said, grabbing a pencil off the desk. "Who doesn't like us, or more specifically, Phoebe?"

"Rockwood's partner," Erica suggested.

"Isn't he in jail?" Scott asked.

"Well, yes," Erica said. "But Rockwood was supposed to be in jail, and he still managed to come after me before."

"Heh, yeah, believe me, I know," Remington said. "I still have the scar on my arm to prove it."

"Sorry," Erica replied. "I didn't mean for you to get involved."

"Don't apologize," Remington replied. "One, it wasn't your fault in the least. And two, this scar looks super cool."

"Sure does," Scott said. "Okay, so Rockwood's partner." He scribbled down the name onto his pad. "Wasn't he an ex-police officer?"

"I think so," Josephine said. "Or maybe my dad - I mean Rockwood - was the police officer. I don't remember."

"It's alright," Scott said. "What other enemies do we have?"

"Maybe we should consider the Huntsmen as a potential enemy," Josephine suggested, her brow furrowed in thought. "They were involved in that whole mess with the kidnappings, and they definitely have a grudge against our families."

Scott looked up from his notepad, intrigued. "That's a good point. Because they're still out there, it's possible they could be involved in this, especially if they want to send a message. But do we know if they're even connected to this kind of attack?"

"They could be," Remington replied, her voice steady. "They're unpredictable and dangerous. If they've found a way to target us again, we need to be prepared."

"Right," Scott said, jotting down "Huntsmen" next to Rockwood's partner. "So we have two potential threats already. Let's keep brainstorming. Who else could have a motive against Phoebe or our families?"

"I think those are the only two enemies we have to worry about right now," Erica said, crossing her arms as she leaned back in her chair. "Rockwood's partner and the Huntsmen seem like the most likely suspects. We should focus on gathering information about them before we start looking elsewhere."

Scott nodded, jotting down Erica's thoughts. "That makes sense. We need to dig deeper into their backgrounds and see if they have any recent connections to Phoebe or the rest of us. If we can find any leads, it might help us figure out who's behind this."

Remington leaned in, her expression serious. "Let's start with Rockwood's partner. If he's still in jail, that could give us a time frame for when he might have been involved in something like this. But we also need to look into the Huntsmen's activities and see if there's been any news about them resurfacing."

"Great idea," Scott said. "I can check online for any news articles or forums discussing Rockwood's partner or the Huntsmen. Maybe we can find something that connects them to Phoebe."

Just then, the library door swung open, and Raven walked in, her brow raised in curiosity. "Hey, what are you guys up to?" she asked, glancing at the serious expressions on their faces.

The four friends exchanged uncertain glances, each weighing whether to share the gravity of the situation with her.

"Who's this?" Remington asked, eyeing Raven curiously.

"Oh, uh, Remington, this is Raven. Raven, this is Remington," Erica said. She gestured to Scott and Josephine. "You've already met Scott and this is Josephine, Remington's younger sister."

"Oh, well, it's nice to meet you guys!" Raven's excited expression shifted to one of concern, when she noticed that everyone's expressions had changed after she had asked what they were up to. "Is everything okay? You all look like you've seen a ghost."

Finally, Scott cleared his throat and said, "We're just... looking into something that happened to a friend of ours. It's kind of serious."

Erica hesitated for a moment before deciding to fill Raven in. "Well, it's about Phoebe. There was an incident at her house, and we think it might be connected to some people we're worried about."

Raven's eyes widened. "Oh no, is she alright?"

"She's in the hospital," Erica replied, almost whispering. "We're trying to figure out who might be behind it."

Raven nodded, her demeanor shifting to one of determination. "I want to help. What can I do?"

Scott smiled slightly, appreciating her willingness to join them. "Well, we were just brainstorming potential suspects. If you have any ideas or information, we'd love to hear it."

With that, Raven pulled up a chair and joined the group, ready to dive into the investigation alongside her new friends.

. . ❧ . .

PHOEBE LAY AWAKE IN her hospital bed, staring at the ceiling. There wasn't a whole lot of entertainment in her hospital room, save for the TV and the few magazines that were at her bedside, neither of which piqued her interest in the slightest.

"I wonder which one is more boring," she said aloud. "The jail cell or this hospital?" Sighing, she reached over for her phone and checked to see if anyone had texted her. There were a few texts from her friends, asking if she was okay, which Phoebe appreciated, but nothing about whether or not they had found the person who had planted the bomb in her house.

Phoebe gazed up at the TV, which seemed to be playing some form of action-romance tv show, and she looked for the remote to change it to something more...educational. To her dismay, she couldn't find anything. Disappointed and extremely bored, Phoebe set the remote back down on the table and looked at the clock. It was 4 PM; she'd missed an entire day of school.

Feeling restless, she swung her legs over the side of the bed and sat up. As she was doing so, a wave of pain shot through her abdomen, causing her to wince and clutch her side. The discomfort was a stark reminder of what she had endured, and she felt an overwhelming wave of frustration wash over her.

"Ugh, this is ridiculous," she groaned, feeling the exhaustion from the pain begin to take hold. The sterile smell of the hospital filled her senses. "I can't just lay here," she muttered to herself, determination bubbling up inside her. She needed to know what was happening outside those four walls, especially concerning the investigation into the bomb.

With a sigh, she leaned back against the pillows, closing her eyes as she tried to steady her breathing and push through the discomfort. "I can't believe this happened to me," she murmured, letting her mind drift to thoughts of her friends and what they might be doing right now. She hoped they were safe and figuring things out without her.

As she lay there, Phoebe's mind raced with thoughts of her friends. She couldn't shake the worry that someone was targeting them, too. The more she thought about it, the more restless she became.

"Maybe I can give them a call," she said to herself, biting her lip in contemplation. But as she thought about it, she realized that she didn't want to worry them further. They already had enough on their plates dealing with the aftermath of the bomb.

Suddenly, the door creaked open, and a nurse walked in, her smile warm and reassuring. "How are we feeling today?" she asked, checking the monitors beside Phoebe's bed.

"Like I just got blown up," Phoebe replied, forcing a small smile despite the pain still gnawing at her abdomen.

The nurse chuckled softly. "Well, considering what you went through, that's understandable. Just remember, healing takes time. Do you need anything? Water? A blanket?"

Phoebe shook her head. "I'm okay, thanks. Just trying to keep my mind off things."

The nurse nodded, her expression shifting to one of understanding. "That's a good plan. Just focus on your recovery for now. Your friends are worried about you, but they'll be back as soon as they can."

"Yeah, I know," Phoebe said, her heart aching at the thought of them. "I just wish I could be out there with them, helping figure this out."

The nurse patted her hand gently. "You will be, just not yet. For now, rest. I'll check on you later." As the nurse left, Phoebe gazed out the window, watching the winter landscape outside. The trees were bare and the sky was a dull gray, mirroring the heaviness in her heart. She thought of her friends and their determination to uncover the truth behind the attack. "I just need to get better," she murmured to herself, feeling a flicker of hope ignite within her. "I'll find a way to help."

*I wonder...*she thought. She picked up her phone and gave Scott a call.

As the phone rang in her hand, Phoebe felt a mix of anxiety and excitement; she wanted to hear what was going on, even if she was stuck in this hospital bed. After a few rings, she finally heard his familiar voice on the other end. "Hello?"

"Scott, it's me," Phoebe said, her voice a little shaky but determined. "I know I'm not there, but I want to know what's happening. Is there any news about the investigation?"

"Phoebe! I'm so glad you called," Scott exclaimed, relief flooding his voice. "How are you feeling?"

"I'll be okay. I'm just a little bored and in pain," she replied, trying to sound upbeat. "But I need to know what you guys are doing. I can't just sit here and do nothing."

"Well, we've been trying to piece together everything that happened," Scott said, his tone becoming serious. "We think whoever did this had a motive, and we're looking into a couple of suspects."

Phoebe's heart raced. "Suspects? Who?"

"Rockwood's partner and the Huntsmen," Scott explained. "We're trying to find any connections to you or our families. It's really serious, Phoebe."

"I had a feeling it might be connected to the Huntsmen," Phoebe said, her mind racing. "They've always seemed to have it out for us. Do you think they could be involved?"

"We don't know yet, but we're digging into it," Scott assured her. "Just focus on getting better. We'll figure this out."

"I want to help," Phoebe insisted, her determination shining through despite her situation.

"I know, and we'll need your help once you're out of there," Scott replied. "Just hang in there, okay? We're all rooting for you."

Phoebe felt a surge of gratitude for her friends. "Thanks, Scott. I'll rest now, but keep me updated, alright?"

"Of course. We'll be in touch," he promised before they ended the call.

With her heart a little lighter, Phoebe set her phone down and leaned back against the pillows, her resolve solidifying. Even from the hospital, she was determined to be part of the investigation to uncover the truth.

As the group finished their brainstorming session, Scott, Erica, Remington, Josephine, and Raven gathered their things and made their way toward the library exit. The atmosphere was thick with unease, each of them acutely aware of the gravity of the situation involving Phoebe.

Scott held the door open for the others, and as they stepped out into the chilly air, the sharp wind hit them all at once. "Man, it feels even colder than before," Scott remarked, pulling his jacket tighter around himself.

"Great, just what we need," Erica said, her voice laced with sarcasm. "A winter chill to match the mood."

Josephine glanced back at the library, her expression pensive. "I just hope Phoebe is okay. I can't shake the feeling that we need to do something more."

"Trust me, we will," Scott replied, his voice steady. "We'll figure this out together. But first, we need to check in with our families and see what they know."

Raven, who had listened intently to their conversation, nodded in agreement. "And if you need any help, I'm in. I want to make sure Phoebe is safe too."

Remington smiled at her determination. "Thanks, Raven. It's good to have you on board. We can use all the help we can get."

As he walked down the street, his breath visible in the cold air, Scott's mind raced with possibilities. He couldn't help but think of the implications of their investigation and how it might put them all in danger. "We need to be careful who we talk to about this," he said. "We don't want to tip anyone off."

"Agreed," Erica said, her brow furrowing. "But we also can't keep this to ourselves for too long. Phoebe deserves to know that we're doing everything we can to protect her."

"Right," Josephine added. "We should also think about how to keep her safe once she's out of the hospital. If whoever did this is still out there, we need to be prepared."

Remington chimed in, "I can help with that. Maybe we can come up with some sort of plan or strategy to keep her safe when she gets back home."

"Isn't that the polices' job?" Raven asked. "I mean, I know we want to help Phoebe ourselves, but I feel like we should leave some things up to the police."

"Yes and no," Scott said. "There's only...5 police officers that work in Greensboro ever since Winston turned corrupt. So it's hard for them to not only protect Phoebe, but also try and figure out who set the bomb."

"I see," Raven replied. "But what exactly can we do? We don't have any of the skills, equipment, or materials they usually have at a police station."

"Well, no, we don't," Scott said. "But you don't necessarily need any of those things."

Raven raised her eyebrows. "It helps."

"Sure does - but we'll have to do the best we can without it," Scott shrugged. "Alright, here's my street - see y'all later." Scott waved goodbye to the group and headed towards his house.

As he got closer to his front steps, he noticed a small package sitting on the bottom step. At first, he assumed that the package was just something his parents had ordered, but after glancing at the label, he saw that it was addressed to him and not his parents.

Strange, he thought. He didn't remember ordering anything, but he took the package inside after unlocking his door. His parents wouldn't be home for at least another hour, and that assumed that everything went smoothly at the store.

He set the box down on the kitchen counter and went to get something to eat. He pulled an orange out of the kitchen fridge and looked for a box cutter to open the package with.

Wonder if it's a Christmas present from my relative? he thought. The label had no return address, so Scott had no idea who had sent it.

Then again, he thought to himself. *Phoebe did just get blown up with a bomb hidden in a package...maybe I shouldn't open this.*

Scott tossed the box cutter in the air a few times as he wondered whether or not to open it. He didn't hear any ticking sounds from it, and given that it looked as though it had truly been sent through the US Postal Service, he was a little hesitant to believe it could be a bomb.

Eventually, Scott's curiosity got the better of him. He opened the box cutter, intending to cut the tape on the box, but before he did that, he decided it was a good idea to play it safe. He took the box off the kitchen counter and carried it outside to his backyard, where he set it down on the grass.

This way, if there is an explosion, I'll have more room to take cover, he thought, as he sliced open the box. He sighed with relief when he realized that there was no bomb in the package, but rather a somewhat poorly wrapped bag. Scott took the bag out of the box and opened it up, laughing when he realized it was just a bag of cookies.

Scott picked everything up and headed back inside, figuring that the cookies were probably from his aunt or some other relative - most of his family members liked to bake and it wouldn't surprise him if they had sent him Christmas cookies.

Scott unwrapped the bag and stuck his hand inside, intending to pull out a cookie. He felt inside and realized that there was also a small piece of paper stuck inside the bag. He pulled it out and unfolded it on the counter. It read:

Dear Scott,

Surprise! I hope this package brightens your day. I know things have been a bit intense lately with everything going on, and I thought you could use a little sweetness in your life.

These cookies are from my mom's secret recipe, and I can guarantee they're as delicious as they look! Just remember to share a few with your family—don't hog them all!

- Erica

Scott chuckled softly as he read the note, a smile creeping onto his face. "Erica always knows how to brighten my day," he said to himself, feeling a bit of the tension lift from his shoulders.

He grabbed a cookie from the bag and took a bite, savoring the sweet taste as he thought about how he could share them with his friends later. "I'll have to save some for the group," he said, his resolve strengthening as he recalled their conversation about Phoebe. "She's going to need all the support we can give her."

As Scott savored the cookie, a wave of warmth spread through him, momentarily distracting him from the weight of the situation concerning Phoebe. It was soft and chewy, the perfect balance of sweetness and flavor. He closed his eyes for a brief moment, letting the taste linger.

But just as he took another bite, a sudden wave of dizziness washed over him. The kitchen began to spin, and he felt a strange heaviness in his limbs. "What's happening?" he murmured, but the words barely escaped his lips before he stumbled back against the counter.

The room tilted dangerously, and he clutched at the edge of the counter, trying to steady himself. The cookie fell from his hand, the half-eaten piece dropping to the floor.

A rush of panic surged through him as he realized he was losing his balance. In an instant, his vision blurred, and he collapsed to the ground, the world around him fading to black around the edges as he succumbed to unconsciousness.

. . ❧ . .

ERICA HAD LEFT THE company of Remington, Raven, and Josephine and was heading back home, where she assumed her parents would be waiting for her. As she walked down the street, she bumped into a man wearing a thick coat and a large, puffy hat.

"Oh, sorry, sir," Erica said, getting out of his way. "Didn't see you there."

The man stopped walking and turned to look at Erica. Erica didn't recognize him at first, but she quickly realized that it was Remington's father - rather, her birth father.

"Oh, hi, Mr. Cassidy," Erica said to him. "How have you been?"

"Oh, not too bad, not too bad," Mr. Cassidy replied. "Getting back into life now, y'know. Doing my best to recover from all the years I was a deadbeat."

Erica laughed a little. "What brings you to this part of town?" If she recalled correctly, the trailer where Mr. Cassidy resided, and what was Remington's old home, was much further from the center of town.

"Just business," Mr. Cassidy replied. "Actually, I don't know if Remington told you, but I've gotten a new job. Well, not quite yet, but soon."

"Oh, no, I don't think Rem ever told me that," Erica said. "She doesn't talk about you all that much."

Mr. Cassidy smiled, although it was a rather sad smile. "I guess I'm not all that surprised," he said. "Remington and I still have a lot to work through."

Erica nodded slightly. "I'm sure she knows you're trying," she said.

"I sure hope so," Mr. Cassidy replied. "Well, anyway, it was good seeing you again, Erica. Give Remington my best wishes when you see her next."

"Of course," Erica said. She waved goodbye, and the two of them left to go to their respective homes.

As Erica entered her house, she was greeted by Lucy, "Hey, Erica," she said. "Mom and Dad aren't home."

"Oh?" Erica asked. "Where'd they go?"

"Out shopping," Lucy responded simply. "Erica, can you help me with something?"

"Depends what that is," Erica said.

"It's Teddy," Lucy complained. "Everytime I try to do something, he comes in and bothers me. He wants me to pitch baseballs for him in the backyard, and he doesn't seem to understand that it's freezing outside and I just want to finish my experiment."

"That sounds like Teddy," Erica laughed. "I'll talk to him and tell him to leave you alone."

"Thanks, Erica," Lucy said. "I really just never understood how we can be so completely different and still be twins."

Erica chuckled. "Genetics, I guess." She tousled Lucy's hair and headed into Teddy's bedroom, where he was sitting on his bed, tossing a baseball in the air.

"What's up, Teddy?" Erica asked.

"Just Lucy being boring and a nerd, like always," Teddy said, sulking. He threw the baseball up at the ceiling and Erica caught it.

"You can't keep bugging Lucy," Erica said to Teddy, taking a seat next to him on his bed. "She has her own life, and you two don't always share the same interests."

"What life?" Teddy demanded. "She just stays in her room all day. She never does anything fun. She's basically a loser."

"Theodore Feldman, don't talk that way about your sister," Erica said sternly. "Listen, you know why she doesn't play sports like you. It's not her fault."

Teddy looked down at the ground. "I know, I know, but it's just so boring. You're always out with your friends and I never really have anybody to talk to or play with."

"We've gotta get you on a sports team," Erica said. "I'll talk to Mom and Dad about finding a team for you to join, but for now, just...leave Lucy alone. She doesn't bother you to help her with her science experiments, so don't nag her to play sports with you."

"Fine," Teddy relented. "Well, will you at least pitch for me?"

"Sure, in a little bit," Erica said. "Just let me get some food to eat first."

Erica hopped off Teddy's bed and walked into the kitchen. Lucy was also there, holding a test vial filled with some form of liquid and a lighter. She shook the test tube a little bit and then added an eyedropper full of another liquid to the tube.

Erica blinked. "*What* are you doing?" she asked Lucy, opening the fridge and pulling out a loaf of bread.

"Nothing, just trying to create a new soap," Lucy replied, shaking the test tube again.

Erica raised her eyebrows as she sliced the loaf. "A new soap? What's wrong with the bottle we have now?"

"Nothing at all," Lucy answered. "I just wanted to create another."

Erica shrugged. "Whatever," she said. "Just don't kill yourself." Erica grabbed a knife from the shelf next to the window and made a face. "What's that smell?" she asked, putting the knife down on the counter.

"What smell?" Lucy asked.

"I don't know, it smells like...rotten eggs," Erica said. "Are you using sulfur in your dish soap or something?"

"No?" Lucy replied, looking up from her test tube and sniffing. "I don't smell anything except mint, but that's just the scent I'm using for the soap."

Erica smelled the air again and shook her head. "No, I definitely smell something." She walked around the kitchen, trying to pinpoint the location of the smell and suddenly began to cough.

"Erica?" Lucy asked. "Are you alright?"

"Yeah," Erica coughed. "I just choked on air or something..." She took a few quick breaths. "There is something going on here - you sure whatever you're making isn't toxic?"

"Pretty sure," Lucy said. "I don't think any of the chemicals I'm using are dangerous."

"If you say so." Erica picked the knife up again and went to cut herself a slice of bread. "Maybe it's just my imagination."

She cut two slices of bread off from the loaf and stuck the loaf back in the fridge, pulling out a bag of cheese before shutting the door. The smell was still there, and it felt like it was getting more powerful.

"No way it's my imagination," Erica said aloud. "I *know* I smell something..." Tossing the bag of cheese on the counter next to the bread, Erica looked around the kitchen, trying to find *something* that could be causing the smell.

The stove? Erica wondered.

She walked over to the stove and inspected it closely, noting that there were no pots or pans on the burners, and everything appeared clean. "Nope, not here," she muttered to herself, frowning as the smell persisted.

Then she began coughing again. As soon as she began walking around the stove, she began choking.

"What is happening?" Lucy asked, looking over at her, concerned.

"I have no idea," Erica choked out. She stepped away from the stove and grabbed herself a glass of water, chugging it. "There's something in the air."

"I really don't feel anything," Lucy said. "I still don't smell anything except mint."

"It's something over by the stove," Erica stated.

Lucy went over to the stove and smelled the air, just as Erica had done. "There's nothing," she said. "I don't know, maybe my condition is preventing me from smelling whatever you're smelling, but there's nothing."

Lucy shrugged and sat back down at the table, but not before getting a glass of water and pouring it into the solution she was making.

"Last step," she said. "Just have to speed boil it and we, I mean, I should be all done."

Lucy turned on the bunsen burner that the test tube was sitting on and was about to light it, when Erica realized what the smell was.

"LUCY, wait!" she almost yelled, catching Lucy by surprise. She dropped the lighter and it clattered to the floor.

"What, Erica?" she demanded. "I'm almost done here."

"That smell!" Erica exclaimed. "It's propane - come on, we have to get out of here!"

Erica grabbed Lucy's hand, and yelled for Teddy to get out of the house. Teddy came dashing out of his bedroom and asked, "What?! What's going on? And what's that smell?"

"It's propane!" Erica said, as she pulled Lucy out of the house. Teddy followed them and ran out of the house, slamming the door behind them.

"What's the emergency?" Teddy asked, mildly confused.

"There's a propane leak," Erica said, her voice edged with urgency. "One single spark will light that entire house up like a firework."

"Is that why you were choking in there?" Lucy asked.

"Yes," Erica replied. She went over to the propane tank that was leaning against the side of the house and found the valve to shut it off. As she was turning the valve, she noticed that there was a slight hissing sound coming from the pipe leading into the house. She realized that the pipe must have been either punctured or snapped, which was causing the propane to seep into the house.

"That was close," Erica said to Lucy and Teddy as she walked back to where they were sitting. "You two didn't hear anyone messing with the propane tank, did you?"

Lucy and Teddy both shrugged. "I don't know," Lucy said. "There was so much arguing going on in our house that we wouldn't have known anyway."

"Wow," Erica said dryly. "I guess it could have just burst or snapped because of wear..."

Or could it be...the same person who was after Phoebe? Erica wondered silently.

Out loud, she said, "Let me call Mom and Dad and tell them what happened. Dad will have to get someone to fix the piping."

Erica pulled her cell phone out of her pocket and dialed her dad's number. Her dad picked up on the second ring, and Erica explained what had happened.

"Wow, I'm glad you three are okay," Erica's dad said, and Erica could hear the stress in his voice. "That was good thinking, honey."

"Thanks, Dad," Erica said. "I'm going to open all the doors and windows and let all the propane out before we go back inside."

"Good idea," Erica's dad agreed. "Listen, we'll be home in about 30 minutes. I'll take a look at the tank and see what happened."

"Thanks, Dad," Erica said again.

After hanging up, Erica turned to Lucy and Teddy, her expression serious. "Alright, let's make sure we keep a safe distance until Mom and Dad get back. I don't want to take any chances with that gas still lingering around. You two stay here while I go and open some windows."

As Erica walked around the house, opening windows, she couldn't help but think back to how she had bumped into Remington's dad while coming home. It seemed coincidental...but given everything that had happened, she really couldn't be sure. Especially, because Remington's dad had no real reason to be on Erica's block. He had said that he was there for "business", but he hadn't specified what business really meant.

As Erica pushed open another kitchen window, she decided that she didn't want to jump to conclusions. Especially not assumptions about Remington's father.

She shook her head, trying to dispel her worries, and returned to the porch where Lucy and Teddy were waiting for her.

.. ✺ ..

SCOTT'S EYES FLUTTERED open, disoriented as he lay on the cool kitchen floor. The faint sound of the clock ticking in the background seemed distant, almost surreal. His mouth felt dry, and a bitter taste lingered on his tongue. As he tried to push himself up, a wave of nausea crashed over him, and he instinctively turned to his side, retching violently onto the tiles.

The kitchen felt both familiar and alien, the warm glow of the overhead light casting long shadows across the room. He could see the crumpled bag of cookies nearby, a stark reminder of how quickly things had taken a turn. Panic gripped him as he realized he was alone; the house felt eerily quiet.

Just then, the front door creaked open, and Scott's parents stepped inside, their laughter fading as they noticed the scene before them. "Scott!" his mother exclaimed, her voice rising in alarm. She rushed over, her face paling as she took in his pallor and the mess on the floor. "What happened?"

His father followed closely behind, kneeling down beside Scott. "Stay with us, buddy. Can you tell us what's wrong?" His voice was steady but edged with concern.

Scott struggled to focus, his thoughts swimming in confusion. "I... I don't know," he managed to croak, his voice weak. "I think... I think it was the cookies."

His mother's brow furrowed as she glanced at the package.

"Scott. We need to get you to the hospital right now." She gently helped him sit up, her hands steadying him.

He felt a wave of dizziness wash over him again, and he leaned heavily against her for support. "I'm sorry, Mom," he whispered, feeling a mix of embarrassment and fear.

"Don't apologize," she said, her voice firm but soothing. "We just need to take care of you."

With his father's help, Scott carefully got to his feet. He felt unsteady, his legs wobbling beneath him, but he leaned into their support. They guided him through the kitchen out into the cool night air.

As they reached the car, Scott's mother helped him into the back seat, her worry evident in her furrowed brow. His father climbed into the driver's seat, already dialing for directions to the nearest hospital. "Hang in there, Scott," he said, glancing back at him with reassuring eyes.

The car's engine roared to life, and Scott felt the vibrations under him, grounding him in the moment. He closed his eyes, focusing on his breathing as they pulled away from the house. The world outside blurred past, the streetlights flickering like distant stars, and he couldn't shake the feeling of dread that clung to him.

"Just breathe, sweetheart," his mother said from the front seat, her voice a calming anchor in the storm of his thoughts. "We're going to help you. You're going to be okay."

Scott nodded weakly, the warmth of her words wrapping around him like a blanket, even as the fear of what had just happened loomed large in his mind.

· · ❧ · ·

ERICA'S PARENTS RETURNED home, their arms laden with shopping bags filled with groceries.

"Hey, where's the propane leak?" her father asked, his gaze scanning the kitchen.

"Um, it's outside," Erica replied.

As they moved toward the back door, Erica pulled out her phone to distract herself, scrolling through messages until her father's voice broke through her thoughts. "Erica, can you come help us with the propane tank?"

With a sigh, she pocketed her phone and joined them outside. The cool night air hit her face, a stark contrast to the warmth inside. They inspected the tank, her father checking the valves while her mother held a flashlight. Just as they were about to finish up, Erica's phone buzzed in her pocket.

She pulled it out, her heart racing when she saw the caller ID: it was Remington. "I'll be right back," she said, stepping away to answer the call.

"Erica, I just heard from Scott's parents. Scott's in the hospital," Remington said, her voice laced with worry.

"What? What happened?" Erica asked, her stomach dropping.

"I don't know all the details, but they said something about cookies. Can you come to the hospital?"

"Of course. I'll be there as soon as I can," Erica replied, her mind racing with fears for Scott's well-being. She ended the call and rushed back to her parents. "Scott's in the hospital. I need to go now."

Her mother's expression shifted from confusion to alarm. "What happened? Do you know?"

"I don't know," Erica admitted, panic rising in her chest. "Remington just called. We need to hurry."

"Okay, let's go!" her father said, his tone serious as he grabbed his keys and ushered them out the door.

Once in the car, the drive felt interminable. When they finally arrived at the hospital, Erica bolted from the car and rushed inside, her parents close behind. The sterile smell of the hospital hit her, mingling with the anxiety that filled the air. As they entered the waiting area, she spotted Officer Miles and Officer McKinley, already talking with Scott's parents.

"Where's Scott?" Erica asked, her voice barely above a whisper as she approached them.

Officer Miles looked up, his expression serious. "He's being treated now."

Erica looked over to Remington, who said, "Scott said that he received a package of cookies that was supposedly from you," Remington said, her voice shaky. "We don't know if it was related to Phoebe's situation, but it's all too suspicious."

"Did you send Scott any cookies?" Josephine asked, her brow furrowing.

Erica shook her head vigorously. "No, I didn't. I've been at the library all day. I haven't baked any cookies in weeks."

As they gathered their thoughts, a nurse emerged from the hallway, her expression serious. "Are you here for Scott?" she asked.

"Yes, we are," Erica said, stepping forward. "What's going on? Is he okay?"

"He's stable, but we need to keep a close eye on him. We're running tests to determine what caused his collapse," the nurse explained. "But we're concerned about the circumstances surrounding it."

"Please, keep us updated," Remington said, her voice determined.

Just then, Officer McKinley and Officer Miles approached Erica, their expressions grave. "Erica, we need to ask you something," Officer McKinley said, his voice steady but laced with concern. "Did you send Scott cookies? He told us that there was a note with the cookies with your name on it."

Erica's heart raced as she shook her head vigorously. "No, I didn't send him any cookies! I've been at the library all day," she insisted, her voice rising with urgency. "There must be some mistake!"

Officer Miles exchanged a worried glance with McKinley. "We need to know if you had anything to do with this."

"Absolutely not!" Erica exclaimed, a mix of fear and indignation flooding through her. "I would never hurt Scott! This person is just using my name to get to Scott!"

"Alright, I believe you," Officer McKinley said, his demeanor shifting to that of a focused investigator. "In the meantime, stay close to your family and try not to worry. We'll keep you updated on Scott's condition."

As they walked away to confer with Scott's parents, Erica felt a mix of dread and determination. She knew she had to get to the bottom of this—Scott's safety depended on it.

Just then, the nurse emerged from the back, her expression serious as she approached the group. "I wanted to update you on Scott's condition," she said, glancing around at the worried faces. "After running our tests, we found traces of poison in the cookies he ingested."

"P-Poison?" Josephine stuttered, her eyes widening in shock.

The nurse nodded solemnly. "It appears that whatever he ate contained a toxic substance."

Erica felt a cold wave of fear wash over her as she exchanged glances with Remington and Josephine, their expressions mirroring her alarm. "Is he going to be okay?" Erica asked, her voice trembling slightly.

"We think so," the nurse reassured them. "He's awake, but he's weak. We need to monitor his condition closely. The sooner the police identify the poison, the better chance we have of treating him effectively."

"When can we visit him?" Josephine asked.

"We don't know yet," the nurse said. "Right now, it's best if only family members visit him. It's just less stress and chaos surrounding him."

Josephine nodded and the three girls each took a seat in the waiting room. "So, are we going to stay here until they let us visit Scott?" Remington asked.

Erica shrugged. "I can't believe this person framed me," she said drearily. She looked up at the ceiling and watched as one of the fluorescent lights flickered. "I would *never* try to hurt Scott. If he thinks I sent him those cookies..."

Remington put her hand on Erica's shoulder. "Erica, listen. I'm sure Scott knows that you didn't send those to him. Trust me, he knows."

"Thanks Remington," Erica responded. She sounded unconvinced, but in her heart, she knew that Remington was most likely right. She just felt terrible that the real criminal had used her name to lure Scott into a false sense of security.

Erica glanced at the clock, and then at her phone, wondering if her parents would be expecting her back soon. They'd dropped her off at the hospital, since they didn't want to leave Lucy and Teddy alone at home, asking her to text them when she needed to be picked up. They hadn't texted her at all, so she assumed that they were busy dealing with the propane leak, or trying to calm down Lucy and Teddy.

"Oh yeah," she said out loud. Josephine and Remington turned to look at her. "There was a propane leak at my house earlier."

Remington looked intrigued. "A propane leak? How'd it happen?"

"I don't know," Erica replied. "I just smelled rotten eggs, and I couldn't figure out where the smell was coming from. It's a good thing I realized what it was before Lucy blew the whole house up."

"What?" Josephine asked. "Did she start the propane leak?"

"Uh, no," Erica laughed. "But she was about to light a lighter for one of her science experiments. And if I hadn't known the smell was propane, she would have blown us all to kingdom come."

"No kidding," Remington said. She was silent for a bit, and then she asked, "So do you think it was just a coincidence?"

"I don't know what to think," Erica replied. "Especially because..." Erica hesitated to bring up seeing Mr. Cassidy by her house to Remington.

"Because what?" Remington demanded, leaving her no choice but to answer.

"It's just..." Erica paused for a minute, then rambled off a group of incomprehendable words causing Remington to raise her eyebrow.

"What?" she asked. "Speak slower."

Erica sighed. "I saw your dad by my house a few minutes before I realized that there was a leak in the propane tank."

"My dad?" Remington asked. "You mean, my birth father?"

"Yes," Erica nodded. "I talked to him for a little bit, and I asked what he was doing there. He said it was just business."

"Business?" Remington asked. "What business?"

"He didn't say," Erica said. "I don't know...I don't want to accuse your dad of anything; I just thought it seemed a little strange that he was there so randomly."

Josephine turned to look at Remington. "Your dad would never do something like that, right? I thought you two were building your relationship."

"We are, we are," Remington said. "And he's actually trying - well, at least he seems to be." Remington sighed. "Look Erica, I don't know what my dad was doing there, but I really don't think he had anything to do with the attacks on you guys. I just don't see him doing that - not at this point."

"I don't either, Remington," Erica replied. "But if there's anything that I've learned from everything that's happened to us, very few things are coincidental."

Remington was about to respond when the nurse entered the waiting room. "I have good news," she said to the three of them. "Your friend is stable; you're more than welcome to visit him now."

"Yes!" Remington exclaimed, a little too loudly. The nurse chuckled and said, "Also, he requested to see..." The nurse checked her clipboard. "Erica Feldman alone. Which one of you is that?"

Remington and Josephine looked at Erica. "Alone?" Erica asked. "Why's that?"

"I don't know - he just requested that," the nurse said, guiding the three girls down the hallway and to Scott's room.

"Should I go first?" Erica asked.

Remington nodded. "Yeah. He wanted to see you alone." Erica pushed open the door to Scott's room and stepped inside, carefully closing the door behind herself.

As she stepped into the room, she found Scott lying in the hospital bed, looking pale and weak but awake. His eyes locked onto hers, and she could see a mix of confusion and hurt in his expression. "Erica," he said hoarsely, his voice barely above a whisper, "why would you send me those cookies?"

Her heart sank at his words, the weight of his accusation crushing her. "Scott, I didn't send you any cookies!" she exclaimed, moving closer to the bed. "I would never do something like that. You have to believe me!"

"But the note was signed by you - it was your handwriting!" Scott pressed, his brow furrowing in distress. "Why would you do this to me? I thought we were friends."

Overwhelmed by a torrent of emotions, Erica felt her throat tighten as tears streamed down her cheeks, blurring her vision of Scott's frail figure. The weight of his accusation felt like a heavy stone in her chest, suffocating her. In a moment of desperation, she turned away from him, her heart racing, and bolted out of the hospital room. The sterile hallway felt suffocating as she sprinted past startled nurses and patients, her sobs echoing in the air.

"Erica, wait!" Remington called out, her voice laced with concern, but Erica couldn't bear to look back. She pushed through the double doors leading to the waiting area, the bright lights stinging her eyes as she hurried toward the exit, her breath coming in ragged gasps. All she could think about was the betrayal that now hung between her and Scott and the weight of his disappointment clawing at her insides. The sound of Remington's footsteps behind her urged her to run faster. She couldn't stop. She needed to escape the weight of Scott's words and the heartbreak they brought with them.

Erica ran and ran, her mind a chaotic whirlwind, not caring where her feet were taking her as long as she could escape the suffocating atmosphere of the hospital. It wasn't until her breath came in heaving gasps and her legs felt like lead that she finally stopped, collapsing onto grass.

As Erica took a moment to catch her breath, she looked around, her surroundings slowly coming into focus.

Where am I? Erica wondered, looking around her.

• • ❧ • •

REMINGTON CALLED OUT for Erica outside the hospital's main doors, her voice filled with urgency. But when there was no response, she quickly ran back through the hospital, her footsteps echoing in the hallways and the echo of Erica's sobs still ringing in her ears.

She slammed Scott's door open, the hinges creaking with the force of her entry. "Scott!" she demanded, her voice fierce. "What did you say to Erica to make her so upset? You need to tell me right now!"

Scott was taken aback, his expression shifting from shock to confusion as he processed Remington's urgency. "I... I just asked Erica why she would send me those cookies," he stammered, his brow furrowing. "I thought we were friends."

Remington's frustration boiled over, her eyes narrowing as she shot back, "Friends don't accuse each other of trying to hurt them, Scott! Do you really think Erica would hurt you? Are you serious right now? She's been there for you through everything, and this is how you repay her? You should have trusted her instead of jumping to conclusions!"

"Remington, calm down," Josephine said. "And Scott, I'm sure Erica didn't send you those cookies. You can't honestly believe that she'd do something like that."

Scott coughed gravely, and said, "B-but the note. It was her handwriting - it had her name on it. All signs pointed to her."

"Come on Scott, don't be so dense!" Remington exclaimed. "You of all people should know how easy it is to fake someone's handwriting. Remember that note that Bert used to frame you?"

"You're right," Scott said, sighing. "I don't know what I was thinking...I messed up."

"You owe Erica an apology," Josephine said. "You just accused your best friend of trying to murder you - do you know how insane that sounds?"

"I know," Scott replied. "At least, now that I think about it. Where is she?"

"I don't know," Remington answered dryly. "She ran off crying without telling us where she was going."

"Oh no," Scott said. "Can you two *please* find her and tell her how sorry I am?"

Remington nodded. "Yeah, we'll look for her. And Scott...maybe think twice before you go ahead and accuse your best friend of murder."

• • ❧ • •

"HEY, WHAT'S WRONG?" a familiar voice rang out, breaking Erica's trance. It was Raven, and Erica quickly realized that she was sitting in the playground, a few feet away from the basketball courts.

Erica took a deep breath, her voice trembling as she explained, "I just had a really awful conversation with Scott. He's in the hospital and he accused me of sending him poisoned cookies. He thinks I was trying to hurt him. I can't believe he'd think that of me."

Raven's expression shifted from concern to disbelief as she stepped closer. "What? That doesn't make any sense, Erica. Despite the little time I have known you, I know you would never do something like that!"

Erica nodded, grateful for Raven's support, but the weight of the situation still hung heavily in her chest.

"I just feel so betrayed, Raven," Erica admitted, her voice cracking as she fought back tears. "Scott is my friend, and to think he could believe I would hurt him like that—it's tearing me apart. I've always been there for him, and now it feels like everything we had is crumbling because of one misunderstanding. It's like he doesn't even know me anymore." She buried her face in her knees, overwhelmed by a mix of anger and sorrow.

Raven knelt beside her, placing a comforting hand on her back. "Erica, listen to me," she said gently. "You know who you are, and you know what kind of person you are. Scott's reaction was extreme, and it doesn't define you. You've always been kind and supportive. This is his issue, not yours."

As Erica looked up, she saw the sincerity in Raven's eyes, and it gave her a small sense of relief. "I just wish he would have trusted me," she murmured, wiping her eyes with the back of her hand.

. . ⚜ . .

REMINGTON AND JOSEPHINE stepped out of the hospital, the weight of worry pressing on their shoulders as they scanned the surrounding area. Remington and Josephine walked past the hospital, the police station, Erica's home, and then Phoebe's house—just a short distance from the school. They exchanged worried glances, hoping to find Erica soon. They walked over to the school parking lot, and as they rounded the last corner to the back of the school, the familiar sight of the playground came into view.

The fading light of the evening cast a warm glow over the empty playground, and as they approached, Remington and Josephine noticed Raven sitting with Erica on the grass near the basketball court, deep in conversation. Relief washed over Remington as she quickened her pace.

"Erica!" Remington called out. Erica turned and looked over at Remington and Josephine in the distance. The two of them approached Erica and sat down next to her and Raven.

"Scott says he's sorry," Josephine said to Erica. "He didn't mean to blame you."

"Really?" Erica replied, her voice barely above a whisper.

"Honestly, he felt terrible about it," Remington said gently, placing a reassuring hand on Erica's shoulder. "He just needs a moment to process everything, but I believe he truly regrets what he said."

Josephine added, "We all make mistakes, and he just needs time to realize how wrong he was."

"Do you want to go back to the hospital and talk to him?" Remington asked, looking at Erica with concern.

"Okay," Erica said, her voice steadier now as she wiped away the last of her tears. With a determined nod, she stood up, and began walking back to the hospital, leaving Raven with Remington and Josephine.

As they pushed through the hospital doors, Erica's parents rushed over, concern etched across their faces. "Erica, are you okay?" her mother asked. "We got a call from Scott's mom—she said she saw you run out of the hospital crying."

"I'm fine," Erica replied, taking a deep breath to steady herself. "I just want to talk with Scott privately."

"Alright, we'll wait for you here," her father said, exchanging a worried glance with her mother as they stepped aside to give Erica space.

Erica took a deep breath and approached Scott's room, her heart pounding in her chest as she raised her hand to knock on the door. The nurse opened it for her, and she stepped inside, the air thick with tension.

"Hey," Erica said softly, trying to keep her voice steady despite the whirlwind of emotions swirling within her. As she looked at Scott, she noticed the weariness etched on his features. She could see he was struggling to reconcile the hurt he had caused her with the pain he was feeling himself.

"Erica," Scott replied, his voice hoarse as he tried to sit up a little straighter. "I'm so sorry about what I said. I didn't mean it. I just... I was confused and scared." His eyes searched hers, desperate for understanding.

Erica felt a mixture of anger and sadness welling up inside her. "Scott, how could you think I would do something like that?" she asked, her voice trembling as she took a step closer to his bedside. "You're my friend. I would never hurt you, let alone try to poison you. I can't believe you would jump to that conclusion so easily."

Scott's brow furrowed, and he looked down at his hands, the guilt washing over him more. "I know, I know. It was a stupid mistake. I saw the note and... I panicked. I should have trusted you."

Erica's heart ached as she watched him struggle with his emotions. "It just hurts, Scott," she admitted, her voice breaking. "You mean a lot to me, and to think you believed I could do something so awful... it feels like our friendship is hanging on by a thread right now."

"I understand," he said, his voice low and sincere. "And I hate that I made you feel this way. I was so focused on my own fear that I didn't even consider how it would affect you. I should have allowed you to speak first instead of jumping to conclusions. You mean too much to me for me to ever want to hurt you."

Erica wiped away a stray tear that had escaped down her cheek, feeling a flicker of hope amidst the pain. "I just wish you would have talked to me before accusing me. It's like you don't even know me anymore."

Scott reached out, his hand trembling slightly as he extended it toward her. "Please, Erica, can we start over? I promise to do better. I don't want to lose you over a misunderstanding. You're my best friend, and I can't imagine my life without you in it."

Her heart softened at his words, and she took his hand, feeling the warmth of his palm against hers. "I don't want to lose you either," she said, her voice steadier now. "But it's going to take time to rebuild that trust. I need to know that you'll believe in me, if something like this happens again."

"I will," Scott promised earnestly, squeezing her hand gently. "I'll do whatever it takes to show you that I trust you. Just please don't give up on me."

In that moment, the weight of the world seemed to lift slightly, the air between them shifting from one of accusation to understanding. Erica nodded, a small smile breaking through her tears.

As they sat together in the quiet of the hospital room, a sense of hope began to blossom, reminding them both that even amidst misunderstanding, true friendship could endure.

. . ❧ . .

"SO, HOW LONG HAVE YOU been in Greensboro?" Remington asked Raven. "I feel like I should have met you before."

"Just a few days," Raven replied. "I don't actually live here - I live with my aunt and uncle in Smithfield."

"Smithfield, hey, I used to live there!" Remington exclaimed. "What are you doing over here?"

"It's a long story," Raven said. "My aunt and uncle are moving across the country to California. But my dad still lives here and if my aunt and uncle move to California, he won't be able to see me ever. So, we're all here to settle things."

"Why don't you live with your dad?" Josephine asked.

"Another long story," Raven laughed. "Y'know, my aunt and uncle never really told me the whole story, but I know it was very chaotic."

"What about your mom?" Josephine asked.

"I have no idea," Raven said. "I really never met her. See, my dad used to come visit me when I was younger, and then when I turned three, his visits slowed down, and then eventually, he didn't come at all. At least, that's what my aunt and uncle tell me. They never really had a very high opinion of my dad."

"How old are you?" Remington asked curiously.

"Seventeen," Raven replied.

"Oh wow, so you're a senior?" Remington said surprised. "I thought you'd be closer to my age. I'm 14."

Raven laughed softly. "Nope, 17. Been 17 for a few months actually - but I guess I look young for my age."

"Or I'm just bad at guessing ages," Remington chuckled. A thought came to her mind suddenly, and she asked, "You said you live in Smithfield - do you know Mrs. Ophelia?"

Raven thought for a little while. "Not that I know of...actually, wait, maybe. Is she an elderly lady?"

Remington nodded. "Yeah, she lives on...I don't remember the name of the road, but I know how to get there by heart. Her house is surrounded by a bunch of run-down houses and ugly trailers."

"Yeah, I think I know who you're talking about," Raven replied. "I've talked to her a few times."

The three sat in silence for a while, staring up at the sky and enjoying the cool weather, until Raven said to Remington and Josephine, "So, what's you guys' story? You're the daughters of the police chief, aren't you?"

"Adopted," Josephine said. "Well, technically, we aren't Officer McKinley's daughters yet. Officer Miles adopted us, and she's going to marry McKinley. Which means we'll officially be Officer McKinley's daughters."

"Cool, a wedding!" Raven said. "Last time I heard of one of those was when my neighbor got married...and then they disappeared 2 weeks later."

"Wow...that's...actually, that sounds like Smithfield," Remington said, half-laughing. "Not surprising, I guess."

"Yeah...nobody knows where they went, but they probably just moved away without telling anyone." Raven paused for a moment, then asked, "So, are you two biological siblings?"

Josephine shook her head. "Nope, only by adoption."

Raven nodded, acknowledging what Josephine had said. "I don't mean to pry, but do either of you know what happened to your biological parents?"

"Eh, technically," Remington said. "Actually, my dad still lives here, and I talk to him a lot. He used to be a deadbeat, drunk all the time, but he's gotten his life back together for the most part. And, well, my mother? I don't know what became of her. She abandoned my dad, and I don't think anyone's heard from her since."

"Oof, I'm sorry," Raven said. "I know how that feels."

"It's fine," Remington said. "My mother was never really part of my life. Most of the time she was off gambling, or at least that's what I assumed that she was doing. Because most of the time she would disappear, she'd come back empty-handed, get into a huge fight with my dad, and then occasionally she would come home with her hands full of cash. Which my dad spent on liquor within the next week."

"Wow..." Josephine broke in. "You never really told me that part of your life."

"I've probably mentioned it before," Remington said. "But I don't think I've really gone into depth about it. I mean, what I just said isn't even half of everything, but it's probably best if nobody hears it."

"Maybe," Josephine said. She looked like she was about to say something else when Raven asked Josephine, "What about you?"

Josephine hesitated, before saying. "It's a hard story to tell."

"I understand," Raven said. "Like I said, I don't mean to pry...if you don't feel comfortable telling me, that's fine."

"Yeah, maybe some other time, I guess, when I'm more open about it," Josephine said. "I just don't like talking about it as of now."

Remington checked her watch, then said, "It's getting a little late - we should probably check in with Phoebe and Scott, and then head home."

"Yeah, me too," Raven agreed. "My aunt doesn't like me to be out that late - especially in this town, since I don't know that many people well."

The three of them stood up and Raven offered Remington and Josephine a hug. "Take care, Raven," Remington said, as the two of them hugged. "I'll see you around."

They all waved goodbye, and each headed their respective ways, hoping to get home before the hour reached double digits.

Christmas Eve, 1 day before Christmas.

As the hospital doors swung open, a wave of warmth and joy washed over the gathered friends and family. Without hesitation, the group rushed forward, enveloping Phoebe in a tight embrace.

"Thank goodness you're finally out of the hospital!" Erica exclaimed.

Phoebe smiled, her heart swelling with gratitude as she felt the comforting presence of her friends surrounding her, a stark contrast to the loneliness she had experienced during her recovery.

"I missed you all so much," Phoebe said, her voice a bit shaky but filled with genuine warmth, as she returned their embrace, grateful to be back among them. Then she looked around the group and asked, "where's Scott?" with a hint of concern, noticing his absence among the crowd.

"He's in the hospital, too," Erica replied, her voice turning serious as she explained the situation, while Remington and Josephine quickly chimed in to share the details of what had happened and how Scott had collapsed after eating cookies that were poisoned.

"Do you know when Scott will be released?" Phoebe asked, her voice filled with concern as she looked at her friends, hoping for some good news.

Erica, Remington, and Josephine exchanged uncertain glances before Erica replied, "We're not sure. They haven't given us any updates yet."

Phoebe nodded. "Let's go ask the nurse." The group made their way to the front desk in the waiting area.

"Excuse me," Phoebe said, her voice steady. "We're here for Scott Ryder. Can you tell us when he might be released?"

The nurse looked up, "Let me check on that for you," she said with a reassuring smile. She turned to a nearby computer and began typing, her fingers flying over the keys as she searched for Scott's information.

After a few moments that felt like an eternity, the nurse turned back to them. "Thank you for your patience. Scott is currently undergoing some additional tests to assess his condition. If everything goes well and he responds positively to treatment, he might be released by the end of today."

As the nurse finished explaining Scott's condition, Erica felt a wave of relief wash over her. "That's good to hear," she said, her voice lightening as she exhaled, and Phoebe nodded in agreement.

After a few more moments of discussion, Erica's thoughts began to drift toward home. "I think I'd like to go home now," she announced. "I want to prepare some soup for Scott. It might help him feel better."

"Great idea!" Phoebe replied, her face brightening at the thought. "He'll appreciate that."

With their plan in mind, Erica and the group said their goodbyes, promising to return later for updates.

As Erica stepped into her house, she was greeted by the familiar scents of pine and cinnamon, the warm glow of holiday lights draping the living room in a cozy ambiance. However, a subtle sense of unease crept into her heart as she called out, "Mom? Dad?"

The living room was quiet, the festive decorations twinkling softly, but the stillness felt unsettling. Erica moved further into the room, her eyes scanning the space. The Christmas tree stood proudly in the corner, adorned with ornaments and tinsel, but something caught her attention on the floor beneath it.

Kneeling down, she noticed a delicate glass ornament lying on the carpet. "How did this fall?" she wondered, reaching for it. As her fingers brushed against the cool glass, a sudden jolt of electricity surged through her body, catching her completely off guard.

"Ah!" she gasped, her muscles tensing as the shock coursed through her.

Her vision blurred, and panic gripped her as she struggled to stay on her feet. But before she could comprehend what had happened, she lost her balance and collapsed to the floor, unconscious.

Meanwhile, Remington and Josephine had decided to give Erica one of Officer Miles' soup recipes. As they approached the front door, they exchanged light-hearted remarks about upcoming Christmas festivities. Josephine's eyes caught the slightly ajar door, her brow furrowing in concern. "Do you think she left it open on purpose?" she asked, a hint of worry creeping into her voice.

"I don't know, but we should check on her," Remington replied, stepping forward and gently pushing the door open wider. As they entered, they were immediately struck by the eerie silence that filled the house.

"Erica?" Remington called out, but her voice echoed back, swallowed by the stillness.

As they ventured further inside, Josephine caught sight of Erica lying motionless on the living room floor, just beneath the tree.

But as they approached, a shadow shifted in the corner of the room. A figure wearing a mask suddenly emerged, looming over Erica's unconscious form. Panic surged through Remington as she instinctively lunged toward the masked intruder, tackling them in a desperate attempt to protect her friend.

The struggle was brief but intense. The masked person fought back, and in a swift motion, they produced a small device that emitted a powerful shock. Remington gasped as the electricity coursed through her body, forcing her to release her grip and stumble backward.

"Remington!" Josephine shouted, paralyzed with shock as she watched her sister fall to the floor, disoriented. The masked figure turned their attention to Josephine, who stood frozen in fear, her breath caught in her throat.

"Josephine, run!" Remington managed to cry out, but it was too late. The masked figure advanced, and with a flick of their wrist, they activated the device again, sending another jolt of electricity toward Josephine. She felt the shock course through her, her body seizing as she fell to the ground, darkness closing in around her as the world faded away.

The masked intruder swiftly grabbed Remington and Josephine, their bodies limp from the electric shocks, and dragged them toward the doorway. Erica, still groggy and struggling to regain her senses, caught a glimpse of the scene unfolding before her. With a weak but desperate effort, she called out, "Remington! Josephine!" Her voice was barely a whisper, just loud enough to escape her lips but not loud enough for the intruder to hear. She watched helplessly as her friends were dragged away. With surprising strength, the intruder maneuvered the sisters into the back seat of a waiting car parked at the side of the house. The door slammed shut with a heavy thud, and the intruder jumped into the driver's seat, starting the engine with a roar. Erica heard the car door slamming shut just as she felt the world around her begin to fade back into darkness. As the tires screeched against the pavement, the car sped away from the house.

• • ❧ • •

AS PHOEBE AND HER PARENTS stepped out of the hospital, a sense of relief washed over her, but it was short-lived. When she was close to her home, she caught sight of a car speeding away from Erica's house. Panic surged through her, and without a second thought, she sprinted toward Erica's home.

Bursting through the front door, Phoebe's eyes widened in horror as she found Erica lying motionless on the floor beneath the Christmas tree. "Erica!" she cried, rushing to her side. Kneeling next to her friend, she quickly checked for signs of life, relief flooding her when she felt a faint pulse beneath her fingers.

Just then, Phoebe's parents burst through the door, their faces etched with concern as they took in the alarming scene before them. "Phoebe! What happened?" her mother exclaimed, rushing to her side. Without hesitation, Phoebe looked up at them, her voice trembling as she explained, "I saw a car speed from Erica's home, so I ran inside to see if everything was okay, and I saw Erica on the floor unconscious."

Her father quickly pulled out his phone, urgency in his voice as he dialed 911. "We need an ambulance right away!" He spoke rapidly, relaying the situation to the operator while Phoebe remained by Erica's side, praying for her friend's safety and hoping that help would arrive soon.

· · ✢ · ·

REMINGTON'S EYES FLUTTERED open, and she quickly realized she was tied to a chair, her hands and legs bound tightly. Panic surged through her as she looked around the dimly lit room, trying to make sense of her surroundings. "Josephine!" she called out, her voice filled with urgency, but there was no response from her sister, who was slumped unconscious in the chair next to her.

Just then, a figure stepped forward from the shadows, and Remington's breath caught in her throat as recognition dawned on her. It was her mother, the last person she expected to see in such a situation. Confusion and disbelief washed over her. "Mom? What are you doing here?"

Remington's voice trembled as she tried to comprehend the reality of the moment.

Mrs. Cassidy narrowed her eyes, her expression a mix of anger and hurt. "Why did you leave me, Remington?" she demanded, her voice shaking with emotion. "After everything I've done for you!"

Remington's frustration boiled over as she yelled, "What do you mean, 'after everything you have done for me'? You left me! You were never there! You were always gone. You came home with money, and Dad wasted it on alcohol and drugs!"

As Remington continued her rant, her mother shot back, insisting that she at least brought money home, but before their argument could escalate further, Josephine began to stir. Confused at first, she quickly became scared as she realized their predicament, and tears streamed down her cheeks.

The sound of Josephine's cries cut through the tension, causing both Remington and her mother to stop and turn their attention to the younger girl. Mrs. Cassidy walked over to Josephine. Kneeling beside her, she grabbed her chin and made Josephine face Remington. "Why would you leave me to be the sister of this crybaby?" she asked Remington, her voice dripping with disdain as she gestured toward Josephine.

"Because of something you could never understand," Remington said, almost pitying her mother.

"Oh, and what's that?" Remington's mom sneered. "Tell me, what do those *police officers* have that I couldn't give you?"

"Love," Remington said simply. "They loved me - something that you never did and never could do."

"I loved you!" Mrs. Cassidy said, almost in a rageful explosion. "I let you live in my house - I fed you, I clothed you, what more did you want? I should have given you up like the first girl!"

Remington froze. What had her mother just said? "First girl?" Remington asked, softer this time. "What first girl?"

"Oh, your father never told you," Mrs. Cassidy asked with a withering look. "You know, if it wasn't for him...you wouldn't have been here either."

"I had a...sister?" Remington asked.

"No, you never had a sister," Mrs. Cassidy said dryly. "She was never a part of my life, or your father's life, or even your life. She's not your sister - and as far as you know, she never existed. She's a forgotten part of all of our lives."

"She's clearly not," Remington said. "You haven't forgotten her - do you have some regret remaining? Some part of you that wishes you had never given her up?"

"Shut up!" Remington's mother hit her fist on a table next to her. "I know what game you're playing - you won't trick me!"

"I'm not playing any games," Remington said. She looked over at Josephine, who was crying softly now. "Mom, what do you want from me - from us?"

"I want nothing from this useless girl." Mrs. Cassidy grabbed Josephine by the arm and began dragging her to a door. Josephine began to scream and fight back; Remington pulled at the ropes holding her to the chair, and said, "You take your hands off of her now!"

"Gladly." Mrs. Cassidy pulled open the door and shoved Josephine into it, slamming the door shut behind her. "Now it's just you and me - how it was always supposed to be. All your friends...they're the ones that took you away from me."

"Is that why you tried to kill Scott, Erica, and Phoebe? You're insane!" Remington told her mother. "You've always been unstable, but now you've gone completely off the rails."

Remington's mother walked over to Remington and looked her in the face. "Have I?" she asked. "*HAVE I?*"

She began walking in a circle around Remington and said, almost hysterically, "Is it so insane to want my daughter back? Tell me that?! It's only human!" Remington's mother suddenly burst out crying and she fell down on her knees, next to Remington.

"Come back to me, daughter," she begged. "Please...*come back*. It's all I want - all I'm asking."

Remington said nothing, which caused her mother to go into a furious rage. She lifted her hand and grabbed Remington by the jaw, squeezing as tightly as she could. "*Answer me!*" she screamed. "*Answer me, you worthless brat!*"

"No," Remington said simply. Her mother released her hand from Remington's jaw and she took a deep breath.

"You...you don't get to say 'no' to me!" Remington's mom almost shouted. She stood up and looked down at Remington. "If you won't be my daughter again, you're not going to be anyone's daughter!"

• • ⚘ • •

ERICA AWOKE AND FOUND herself lying on a hospital bed, alone. "Hello?" she called out. "Is anyone there?"

The door swung open, and Erica's parent's burst in, along with Phoebe and Raven.

As Erica's parents rushed into the room, their expressions filled with relief, she felt a wave of comfort wash over her. "Erica! Thank goodness you're awake!" her mother exclaimed, rushing to her side.

"What happened? Why did you collapse?" her father asked, concern etched on his face as he knelt beside her.

Erica blinked, trying to gather her thoughts. "I... I was at home, and then I saw an ornament under the tree. When I tried to put the ornament back on the tree, I felt this weird shock, and everything went black," she stammered, her memory still hazy.

Phoebe, standing nearby, frowned with worry. "A shock? Like an electric shock?"

"Yeah, something like that," Erica replied.

"Wait, there was a masked figure in my house," Erica suddenly recalled, her eyes widening in alarm. "I remember seeing them just before everything went dark. Remington jumped on them to try to protect me, and then they shocked her with some kind of device. I think Josephine tried to help too, but then I saw them getting dragged away... and that's when I lost consciousness."

Her heart raced as the memories flooded back, the fear and confusion of that moment crashing over her like a wave. "I couldn't do anything to help them," she said, her voice trembling. "I just watched as they took them."

Phoebe exchanged worried glances with Erica's parents, sensing the urgency of the situation. "We need to tell the police," Phoebe urged. "They have to know about the masked figure and what happened in your house."

"Yes, absolutely," Erica nodded, determination rising within her. "We have to find Remington and Josephine before it's too late."

Just then, Officer McKinley and Officer Miles entered the room, their expressions serious as they approached Erica's bedside. "Erica, I'm glad to see you awake," Officer McKinley said, his tone shifting to one of concern. "We need to talk to you about what happened at your house. Can you tell us everything you remember?"

Erica nodded, and explained once again what happened.

When Erica got to the part where Remington and Josephine were taken, she saw Officer Miles' expression change. She looked like she was about to punch someone.

"Are you okay, Officer Miles?" Erica asked, concerned.

Officer Miles took a deep breath, her frustration evident. "I received a really weird letter a week ago," she said, her voice tense. "It said something like 'I want her back. I will find her.' I threw it away, but I should have known it was serious."

"Amelia, you never told me this," McKinley said. "You should have mentioned this to me - I would have looked into it."

"I know, I know," Miles replied. "But I didn't really see its significance before. It didn't seem very important to me."

Officer McKinley placed a reassuring hand on her shoulder. "Don't beat yourself up for it, Amelia. We'll figure this out."

But then Officer Miles continued, her brow furrowing in thought. "The letter had a name at the end - Samantha."

"Samantha?" Phoebe asked. "Whom do we know that's named Samantha?"

"Nobody comes to mind," Erica said, scratching her head in thought. "Samantha..."

"Well..." Raven started to say something, then stopped.

Everyone turned to Raven, expecting her to say something else. "It's probably not relevant," she stated. "But...I think my aunt once told me that my mom's name was Samantha."

There was silence and Raven quickly added, "But I don't know what my mother would have to do with Remington and Josephine."

"Nothing, but I wonder..." Phoebe stared into Raven's eyes. "Your eyes...I just can't get over how exactly they mirror Remington's."

Raven turned away, a little weirded out. "Yeah...you mentioned that when we first met. But I don't understand why-"

"I do," Erica interrupted. "Raven, tell me...where does your dad live? And what is his name?"

• • ❧ • •

AN EVIL SMILE APPEARED on Remington's mom's face as she began walking around the room. "You'll be my daughter again, even if it's the last thing you do," she exclaimed maniacally.

Remington desperately tried to free her arms from the ropes holding her fast to the chair. "Mom, please, you need to stop this!" she pleaded, her voice trembling with a mixture of anger and desperation. "This isn't the way to fix things! You can't just take us hostage because you feel abandoned!"

Her mother paused, her expression shifting from rage to something resembling sadness for a fleeting moment. "You don't understand," she said, her voice lowering as she stepped closer, her eyes narrowing. "I did everything for you. You chose them over me!"

Tears stung Remington's eyes as she fought to maintain her composure and Mrs. Cassidy's expression darkened, "You will learn to love me again," she spat, her words laced with venom. "One way or another."

She grabbed a can of gasoline that was sitting in a corner, and began to laugh hysterically as she opened the cover. She lifted the can above her head and spread some in a circle around her, before leaning towards Remington, and splashing her with gasoline. The smell made her almost gag and the fumes made her eyes water.

"Mom, you can't do this!" Remington begged. "You have to accept - accept that I'm not your daughter anymore."

"*I* don't have to accept anything!" Remington's mom screamed in return. "*You* just have to become my daughter again.

"It's not going to happen," Remington said, trying to keep her voice calm. "And nothing you do will convince me."

"Ohh, nothing at all?" Remington's mom demanded. She tossed more gasoline on Remington, causing her to choke. "I think you'll change your mind sooner or later!"

"If you kill me...you're not going to accomplish anything," Remington said. "I can't be your daughter when I'm dead."

"You'll only *wish* you were dead," Remington's mother replied evilly. She reached into her pocket and pulled out a match, saying, "If I light this match..." she didn't finish her sentence, but Remington knew what she was going to say.

"I thought you said you weren't going to kill me," Remington said to her dryly.

"I'm not...you're right - nothing I do to you will ever convince you," Mrs. Cassidy said, a sinister look forming on her face. "You've always been too strong-willed...but what about..."

Mrs. Cassidy pulled the door to where she had shoved Josephine open and yanked Josephine out by her arm. "Please," Josephine begged, tears streaming from her eyes. "Don't hurt us."

"Don't," Remington said. "Don't use her to get to me. She's never done anything to you."

"Ah, well then…she's the perfect target." Mrs. Cassidy said. She stepped closer to Josephine, who trembled in fear, her wide eyes filled with tears.

"You see, Remington," Mrs. Cassidy said, her voice dripping with malice, "if you refuse to accept me as your mother, then perhaps witnessing your sister's suffering will make you reconsider. I will not let you go that easily."

"Please, don't hurt her!" Remington cried, her heart racing as she struggled against the ropes binding her. "You can't do this! Josephine has nothing to do with your problems!"

Mrs. Cassidy ignored her pleas, instead focusing her attention on Josephine, who was now shaking uncontrollably. "You think you're safe because you're not my biological daughter? You think you can just walk away from this? No one walks away from me!"

With a swift motion, she pulled Josephine closer, gripping her arm tightly and twisting it as hard as possible. "You're going to help me remind Remington of what family really means," she hissed, her face twisted in a frightening mixture of anger and desperation.

"Stop it!" Remington shouted, her voice breaking. "You're hurting her! You don't have to do this! You can still change! We can talk this out!"

Mrs. Cassidy's expression hardened. "Talk? You think I want to talk? You chose your new family over me, and now I'm going to show you just how wrong that choice was." She reached for the gas can once again, but this time, poured it on Josephine. "Not you, but her!"

As she spoke, she raised the match in her hand, and struck it against the side of the box. The flame flickered ominously in the dim light and Remington's heart began to race, knowing that her mother would not hesitate to drop the match on Josephine. "No! Don't do it!" she begged. "Fine, I will be your daughter! Please don't do anything to her!"

"You will? You will!" Mrs. Cassidy walked back over to Remington. "Thank you, my daughter." She paused for a moment, then whispered. "My Remington Cassidy." She walked over to her, and hugged her as tight as possible.

..⁓..

RAVEN HESITATED FOR a moment before answering, "His name is Richard and he lives in Greensboro. I think he also lives in a trailer. But it is located close to the edge of town, a couple miles before that run-down bar in no-man's land."

Phoebe's eyes widened, "I knew it!" she exclaimed. "Officer Miles, you guys have DNA tests at the station, don't you?"

"Yes?" Miles responded. "I...wait, you don't think..."

"Think what?" Raven asked. "Can someone fill me in?"

"You are - well, I think you are - Remington's sister," Phoebe said. "I mean, I don't know, but it makes sense."

"*What?*" Raven demanded, looking extremely bewildered.

"No, the pieces fit together," Erica said, sitting up in her bed. "Your eyes...your dad's house, even your dad's name is the same - there's no other way to put it."

"This is...insane," Raven said. "My aunt and uncle never told me that I had a sister...neither did my father. Are you sure?"

"Absolutely not," Phoebe said. "I'd be lying if I said I was sure. But - the only way to be sure is to take a DNA test."

"Is Remington's DNA on file?" Erica asked.

Miles nodded. "Yes, it was a requirement when I adopted her."

"It's up to you," Phoebe said to Raven.

"I don't know...this is...look, will this help find Remington and Josephine?" Raven asked.

"Yes...well, no," Phoebe replied. "Actually, Officer McKinley, can we just assume I'm right and go on the basis that "Samantha" is not only

Raven's mother, but also Remington's mother? Why don't we just go talk to Raven's father?"

"Yes, but only if he is willing to help," McKinley replied. "Without solid evidence that he or his wife is involved, we're never going to be able to get a warrant."

"And I really don't know where he lives," Raven said. "I have a general idea, but I haven't been to his house in ages. He always came and visited me at my house."

"Alright, then we go to Remington's father's house," Erica said. "And if they're the same person..." She didn't finish her sentence, but it was very evident what she was going to say next.

. . ✺ . .

MEANWHILE, MR. CASSIDY sat at the edge of his bed, staring blankly at his phone. A message from his estranged wife popped up on the screen, sending chills down his spine. "I got her. I got her back."

"What do you mean; who did you get back?" he typed back, a sense of dread pooling in his stomach.

A few moments later, the reply came: "Our daughter...our beautiful daughter."

Panic surged through him. "What did you do?" he texted back, his fingers trembling as he felt the weight of his past decisions pressing down on him.

His heart raced as he ran into the back of the trailer and grabbed a shotgun from his gun safe; the feeling of the cold metal was a stark reminder of the life he had tried to leave behind. He said to himself, "I will find my daughter, even if it is the last thing I do."

He knew where Samantha would be—an abandoned bar at the edge of town, a place shrouded in memories of neglect and lost opportunities. As he drove through the back roads, he took a deep breath, trying to steady his nerves. *I can't let her hurt my daughter. Not again.*

When he arrived, the bar loomed ominously against the night sky, with its boarded windows and splintered walls. He parked a distance away, heart pounding as he crept toward the entrance. The air was thick with anticipation and fear, but he pushed it aside, focusing on his goal.

Quietly, he approached the back door, counting down in his head. One... two... three! He kicked the door open, the loud bang, followed by the creak of the door's hinges echoing through the empty space.

"SAMANTHA!" he bellowed, as loud as he could. His voice echoed through the empty room as he stormed through the bar, looking for any trace of his daughter or his wife. He knew the bar well - he had been there many times before it had closed, and he frantically searched through every room in the place.

He came up empty - he had ransacked and searched every room, to no avail. "No..." he said aloud to himself. "They must be here. There's no other place."

He looked around the bar and took in all the haunting memories it held. Memories from a distant past. *But is it really so distant?* he thought to himself. It felt like it had only been a few days since he had last gotten drunk...or maybe done even worse things. The town held too many reminders for him - he wondered if he would ever be able to overcome the past which felt as though it was grabbing onto him with iron claws.

But right now, that wasn't what mattered. He had one mission - to find his daughter, and save her from someone who he had once loved dearly. He called out once again for Remington or Samantha, but was met with nothing but the sound of his own echo.

Suddenly, he was reminded of something. There was a place in this bar...a place that had been kept hidden from the police, because of the activities that went on down there. He had spent a shameful amount of time in that area, but now he just needed to remember how to get there once again. He racked his brain for any memory that he had of the place...and suddenly it hit him.

He ran down the hallway, until he came to a mirror just outside the restrooms. He smiled, remembering now; he smashed the mirror with his foot, revealing...nothing.

"No!" he shouted. "This is-this is the place - I remember!" He desperately began searching for some entrance, pounding on the wall in a mad fury.

Where is it?! He continued to bang.

As Mr. Cassidy continued to pound on the wall in a frenzy, his frustration mounting, he suddenly heard a distinct sound—one that resonated differently than the hollow thud of his fists against the wall. It was a muffled bang, like wood striking wood.

He paused, straining to identify the source of the sound. Leaning closer, he pressed his ear against the wall, listening intently. There it was again, a faint thud, accompanied by a low creaking noise. His heart raced as he realized that he might be onto something.

With renewed vigor, he stepped back and began to search the area around the mirror more thoroughly. He ran his hands along the edges of the wall, feeling for any irregularities or hidden mechanisms. His fingers brushed against a small, inconspicuous panel, slightly ajar.

"This has to be it," he murmured to himself, adrenaline surging as he pulled the panel open further. With a swift motion, he shoved it aside, revealing a narrow door concealed behind the mirror. It was an old, weathered door, its paint peeling and its handle rusted, but it felt like a passage to the past he once knew all too well.

The smell of gasoline filled his nostrils as he breathed in the musty air from the long-abandoned room.

"Remington!" he shouted, while running through the narrow doorway. His eyes began to adjust to the dark room, and he realized that he could hear screaming in the distance. He followed the sound and came to another door, from which the screaming was coming from behind.

Taking a deep breath, Mr. Cassidy took his shotgun off of his shoulder, pointed it at the door, and with a swift kick, forced the door open. The scene that met his eyes was not one that he was expecting. His wife was...hugging his daughter, Remington?

Mrs. Cassidy turned away from Remington and faced her husband. "What did you do?" Mr. Cassidy asked in a low voice.

"I got her back!" Mrs. Cassidy almost shrieked. "I got her back! She's mine...she's ours again!"

Mr. Cassidy shook his head. "Samantha, *what did you do*?" he asked coldly.

"Didn't you hear me?!" Samantha said, with almost childish glee. "Don't you want your daughter back?! We'll be a family again, Richard! A family, you hear?!"

"No," Richard replied. "She's not our daughter anymore. We had our chance and we screwed it up. Accept this and live with it."

"Never!" Samantha screamed at the top of her lungs. "All of you; you all want to take her away from me. I'll kill you all - none of you will stand in my way! And we'll start with this one!"

Samantha pulled another match from her pocket and lit it, holding it just a few inches above Josephine's head. "She's dead, just as you all will be as well! Anyone who tries to take my daughter from me!"

Samantha opened her fingers slowly, and time seemed to go in slow motion for Remington. She saw the match begin to fall, and she opened her mouth to scream, but nothing audible escaped. Then, she heard the sound of a shotgun blast, a scream rang out, and time sped up once again.

Her father stood there, shotgun smoking, while her mother lay next to Josephine, clutching her arm in pain. The dreaded match lay on the ground, extinguished and smoking and her father rushed over to Remington and quickly sliced her bonds with his pocket knife.

"Oh, Dad, thank you so much," Remington embraced her father in a heavy hug, before running over to Josephine, who was conscious, but seemed to be in shock.

"Josephine, it's alright, it's over," Remington said to Josephine, putting her hand gently on her shoulder.

"No, it's not!" Samantha stood up, still clutching her arm. "It's not over - you promised you'd be my daughter again! You can't go back on that promise!"

Overcome with blind rage, Remington drew her fist back and punched her mother square in the jaw, causing her to stumble back and look at Remington in horror.

"I'm not your daughter anymore!" Remington shouted. "I'M NEVER GOING TO BE YOUR DAUGHTER AGAIN! LIVE WITH IT!"

"No...you can't - you promised!" Remington's mother said desperately.

"When did I ever say, 'I promise to be your daughter'?" Remington demanded. "I'd said I'd be your daughter again so you wouldn't kill Josephine. You're a psychopath - not someone fit to be a mother!"

"Don't!" Samantha lunged at Remington, but Richard stepped in the way and said, "Respect her decision, Samantha. It's done - it's over."

"You! This is all your fault!" Samantha yelled at Richard. "I had her back - she was mine again, and you-you ruined it!" Samantha tried to attack Richard, but he grabbed her by the arm and said, "You're not the person I married - maybe you never were...but right now - all I see you as is a person trying to hurt my daughter."

Richard pulled a screaming Samantha over to the chair where Remington had been tied to and tied her there. "It's really a shame you couldn't turn your life around," he said. "I remember a time when you were one of the smartest women I knew."

He turned away from the raging Samantha and to Remington, who was helping Josephine up, who was weak, but for the most part, okay.

"Are you two alright?" he asked. When Remington nodded, he said, "I'm sorry this happened - I should have seen it coming and prevented it. I knew your mother was unstable when she left...but I didn't realize it was to this degree."

"It's not your fault," Remington said to her dad. "Don't blame yourself - nobody made these decisions except for her."

"Thank you, Remington," Richard said. He pulled his phone out of his pocket. "I think it's best we call the police now, don't you?"

• • ❦ • •

"WE'RE ALMOST THERE," Miles said, as she drove the car out of the friendly neighborhood streets and into the area where Remington's father lived.

Raven bit her tongue and said, "I know where we are...this is where my father lives. I recognize these houses from when I was last at his house."

"You're sure?" Phoebe asked. "Because this is...well, it's where Remington's father lives."

"I'm positive - this is the same area where *my* father lives," Raven said. "Could this really be possible? Could I really be Remington's sister?"

Phoebe was about to answer, when she was interrupted by McKinley's walkie-talkie. "Chief," Wesley's voice came over the radio. "We know where they are."

The car came to a screeching halt. "Where?" McKinley asked. "And how?"

Wesley gave them the address of the abandoned bar. "We received a 911 call from them. Believe me...this is a story for the ages."

Turning the car around, McKinley sped out of the run-down neighborhood and towards the address Wesley had given him.

• • ❦ • •

MEANWHILE, REMINGTON had a few questions for her father. "Dad, I need to know. Do I have a sister? A biological one?"

Richard looked at Remington and was silent for a while. "Yes," he said. "You have a sister a few years older than you."

"Why-why didn't you ever tell me?" Remington asked quietly. "Who is she?"

"I just...I couldn't ever find the right time or the right words to tell you," Richard said sadly. "It was a heartbreaking experience for me."

"Why did you give her up?" Remington asked.

"Samantha - your mother - she insisted upon it," Richard said. "We were poor - and she knew we didn't have the means to raise a child. I wanted to keep her, but in the end, it just couldn't happen. So, we sent her to live with her aunt and uncle. I guess we figured it was a little better than having her live with strangers, and they didn't live all that far away.

"I tried to visit her every week...but then...things fell apart. Drugs, alcohol - we began to spiral. Then you were born. Samantha wanted to give you to your aunt and uncle as well, but this time I didn't let her. I guess maybe it would have been better for you if I had, given the childhood you had. But once you were born, my visits to our other daughter slowed down...and my mental state deteriorated. Then we moved to the trailer, out of Smithfield, and my visits stopped completely."

Richard wiped away a tear from his eye as he finished his story, but Remington had only one single question remaining. "What's her name?"

"Raven." The answer hit her like a brick.

"R-raven?" she asked. "As in...the Raven that Erica introduced me to? That Raven?"

Richard had a blank expression on his face, so Remington asked, "She looks like me, doesn't she? Long, dark hair? Does she play basketball?"

"Yes to all of the above," Richard replied. "You two have...met before?"

"I-I think so," Remington said. "She said that she lived with her aunt and uncle...and that they were moving away to California and that she was here to work things out with her dad?"

Richard nodded. "You've met her, alright. It's a wonder that it never clicked that you two were sisters...I always thought the both of you could have been twins."

"Wow...but I don't understand," Remington said. "What is there to work out with you?"

"Well, like she said, my brother and sister are moving to California - across the country," Richard explained. "And I don't want to never be able to see my daughter again. So...I'm trying to gain custody of her before she turns 18."

"So, Raven is really my sister? All this time, I had no idea... Do you think she'll want to be part of our family?" Remington looked at her father, searching for assurance.

"Raven's open to the idea...but I don't know that a judge will be," Richard said. "I still don't have a stable job and that's one of the requirements for taking custody of a child."

The two of them were silent for a while, until the door to the room opened, and McKinley, Miles, Phoebe and Raven walked in. "Remington, Josephine, thank goodness you're alright!" Phoebe exclaimed, embracing the two of them in a tight hug. "What happened?"

Remington was going to say something, but turned to look at Raven who was staring directly at Richard. "Dad? What are you doing here?"

"Raven...there's something you should know," Richard started, but Raven held up her hand. "I know what you're going to say."

"You do?" Richard asked. Raven nodded. "Remington is my sister, isn't she?"

Richard smiled warmly. "You two have a lot to get to know about each other..."

Meanwhile, Miles had cuffed Samantha and was taking her out to the cruiser waiting outside. Before she left, Richard held up his hand and said, "My wife is not mentally stable - I doubt jail will do her any good. What she needs is a mental institution to help her regain her sanity."

"I'm sure that's what a judge will rule as well," Miles said to Richard, as she led Samantha out of the bar and into the cruiser. The rest of the people followed behind, leaving the cursed place in the dust and rubble, to hopefully never be seen again.

Christmas Day, 0 days before Christmas

The holiday had finally arrived in full swing, and the home of Miles and McKinley was a festive haven. The air was filled with the mouth watering aroma of a holiday feast, and the atmosphere was electric with laughter and chatter as friends and family gathered to celebrate. The living room was aglow with twinkling fairy lights draped over the mantle and a magnificent Christmas tree standing proudly in the corner, its branches adorned with colorful ornaments that sparkled under the soft glow of the lights.

Erica and Scott arrived together, their breath visible in the crisp, wintry air as they stepped inside. The warmth of the house enveloped them like a cozy blanket, and they were immediately greeted by the joyous sounds of their friends mingling in the adjoining dining room.

"Wow, it looks amazing in here!" Erica exclaimed, her eyes widening as she took in the decorations.

"Yeah, Officer Miles really knows how to throw a party," Scott replied, grinning at her enthusiasm.

As they made their way toward the dining room, Erica felt a surge of happiness at the thought of spending the evening with everyone. Just as they reached the doorway, something caught her eye.

"Wait," Erica said, stopping in her tracks. She looked up and gasped. "Mistletoe!"

Scott followed her gaze and chuckled, a playful smile spreading across his face. "Well, it looks like we have to do something about that, don't we?"

Feeling a rush of courage, Erica turned to face him, her heart racing. "I guess we do," she said, her voice barely above a whisper.

Without thinking twice, she leaned in and pressed a soft kiss on Scott's cheek. "I like you, you know," she added, her cheeks flushing slightly.

Scott's expression shifted from surprise to delight, a broad smile breaking across his face. "I like you too, Erica," he replied, his voice warm and sincere. The moment was a sweet and simple exchange that left both of them grinning as they stepped through the doorway into the dining room.

The dining room was a sight to behold. The long table was beautifully set with a festive red and green tablecloth, adorned with a stunning centerpiece of pine branches, red berries, and flickering candles. The table overflowed with an array of dishes: a perfectly roasted turkey, fluffy mashed potatoes, savory stuffing, vibrant green beans, and a rich gravy that glistened under the candlelight. The scent of freshly baked rolls wafted through the air, and a large bowl of cranberry sauce added a pop of color to the feast.

As they entered the room, they were greeted by the cheerful sounds of laughter and conversation. Remington, Josephine, Raven, and Phoebe were already seated, their plates piled high with delicious food. The camaraderie in the air was palpable, a reminder of the strong bond they all shared.

"Hey, you two! Finally made it!" Remington called out, waving them over to the table. "We were just talking about how much food there is!"

As Erica and Scott took their seats, Amelia appeared from the kitchen, carrying a steaming pot of gravy. "I hope everyone is hungry!" she announced, setting the pot down on the table with a flourish. "I made plenty for seconds!"

"Looks amazing, Officer Miles!" Phoebe said, her voice filled with enthusiasm as she clapped her hands together.

With everyone gathered around the table, the meal began, and laughter filled the air as they passed around the dishes. Erica felt a sense of warmth wash over her as she watched her friends enjoy the feast.

The food was delicious and the conversation flowed easily, filled with stories, jokes, and shared memories of holiday traditions.

At one point, as they were all chatting about their favorite holiday movies, Officer McKinley stood up, raising his glass to get everyone's attention. "If I could have a moment, please," he said, his voice resonating through the room. The chatter gradually quieted, and all eyes turned to him.

"I just want to take a moment to express how grateful I am for each and every one of you. This holiday season is about coming together, and I can't think of a better group of people to celebrate with," he said, his voice warm and heartfelt.

Everyone raised their glasses in agreement. "Cheers!" they all shouted, their voices mingling in joyful harmony.

As the moment of gratitude settled over the table, Remington's father, Mr. Cassidy, cleared his throat, and an air of anticipation filled the room. "I have something important to share as well," he began, his tone serious yet gentle. "I've decided to move away with Raven."

The room fell silent, shock and surprise etched on everyone's faces. Raven looked both nervous and excited, glancing at Remington, who appeared taken aback. "Wait, what? You're moving?" Remington finally managed to say, her voice barely above a whisper.

"Yes, it's true," Mr. Cassidy said, his eyes softening as he looked at his daughter. "We're moving to Virginia - it's not too far from here. But it was because I was able to get a job down there. And once I secured that job...the judge was willing to grant me custody of Raven for the few remaining months before she turns 18.

"I know it's sudden, and I'm sorry," he continued, his tone soothing. "But this is an opportunity for growth for both of us. I'll always be here for you, no matter where we are."

Raven reached for Remington's hand, squeezing it gently. "We'll visit often, I promise," she said, trying to reassure her newly-found sister. "This doesn't mean goodbye forever."

Remington looked up, a small smile breaking through her initial shock. "Yeah, I guess you're right. "I'll hold you to that."

With the tension in the room slowly dissolving, the conversation shifted again. Laughter began to echo as they reminisced about their time together, sharing funny stories and cherished memories. Erica felt grateful for the warmth and love that enveloped them all, a reminder of the friendships that could withstand any challenge.

As the evening wound down, they all gathered around the tree for one final toast and gift exchange. Erica took a moment to appreciate the magic of the season. Surrounded by friends, family, and the promise of new beginnings, she knew that this was a holiday she would always remember—a night filled with love, laughter, and joy.

Epilogue: The Day After Christmas

"Okay Mr. Feldman, you're all set." The repairman stuck his wrench back into his toolbelt and handed Erica's dad a piece of a pipe. "Propane should be back up and running again."

"Thank you very much, Dave," Erica's dad replied, shaking his hand and taking the busted pipe from him.

"No problem - sorry I couldn't come out sooner. Christmas is a heck of a time for your propane to go out," Dave replied, with a cluck of his tongue.

"So, what happened to it?" Erica asked.

"Ya got a leak," Dave answered. "Then again, I'm guessing you already knew that."

"Yeah, I mean how did the leak happen?" Erica asked.

"Your pipe rusted out," Dave answered. "The connection between the stove and the tank just got a hole. Happens a lot with older tanks, since the pipes weren't always built to withstand the cold weather, and they just weaken."

He took the pipe back from Erica's dad and showed Erica the rusty hole in the pipe's connection point. "Right there."

"So, nobody tampered with it or anything?" Erica asked.

"Not as far as I know," Dave replied. "Unless you're admitting to something..."

"No, no," Erica said quickly, laughing. *I guess some things really are just coincidences,* she thought to herself.

"Alright, you guys take care now." Dave set the pipe on the top of the propane tank and gave a wave goodbye, before climbing back into his truck and driving away. Erica watched him leave and as the truck disappeared into the distance, she felt a strange mix of relief and anticipation, knowing that life, unpredictable as ever, was ready to unfold once more.

THE END

• • ❧ • •

Did you love *Presents, Poison, and Peril*? Then you should read *Kidnappers, Killers, and Karma*[1] by Travis Cramer!

[2]

Join the group on their fourth and biggest adventure yet! When Josephine gets kidnapped, Erica is dragged along and it's up to the rest of the group to find out where they are and rescue them from the hands of their kidnappers. Things get more complicated when they learn that perhaps it's not actually Josephine they're after...and the group becomes intertwined in a much bigger plot than they had ever thought possible.

Follow Erica, with her steely determination, Adrian and Phoebe with their logical and rational minds, Scott with his never-ending creativity, Josephine with her never-ending positivity and warmth even in the worst of situations, and finally, Remington, with her semi-ethical, but always practical solutions! The six of them must work

---

1. https://books2read.com/u/47B0qa

2. https://books2read.com/u/47B0qa

together, despite disagreements that spread throughout the group, and take down one of the most dangerous criminals they've ever faced. This story will keep you on the edge of your seat as you read it, biting your nails, anxious to know what happens next. Will it all end well for everyone? Will the criminals be put to justice and will our heroes come out on top? Find out, when you read the fourth story in the Misadventure and Mystery series - Kidnappers, Killers, and Karma!

Read more at https://books2read.com/ap/81Do3O/Travis-Cramer.

Also by Travis Cramer

Misadventure and Mystery
Cars, Computers, and Chaos
Secrets, Suspicions, and Silence
Revenge, Rescue, and Revelations
Kidnappers, Killers, and Karma
Presents, Poison, and Peril

Watch for more at https://books2read.com/ap/81Do3O/
Travis-Cramer.

Also by Marcelina Bratz

Misadventure and Mystery
Presents, Poison, and Peril

About the Author

Travis Cramer is a 17-year-old storyteller with roots in the lively state of New Jersey. At 12, his family traded the hustle and bustle for the quieter charm of Delaware—a shift that left young Travis searching for adventure. With fewer distractions in his new surroundings, he turned to his love of fiction as an outlet for creativity. What started as a simple hobby soon transformed into a mission: to write a full-fledged story, beginning to end. From this spark of inspiration, *Misadventure and Mystery* was born—a series where imagination knows no bounds, and every page brims with excitement and intrigue.

Marcelina Bratz is a 15-year-old girl who has lived in Delaware her entire life. Her love for reading blossomed into a passion for writing after she was inspired by her friend, Travis Cramer. When Travis faced a time crunch while working on a Christmas book, Marcelina jumped at the chance to help as a co-author, marking the beginning of her own writing journey. Outside of writing, Marcelina enjoys ice-skating, playing video games, cooking, and catching up on sleep, embracing a well-rounded life filled with creativity and adventure.